The Mystery at Haunted Ridge

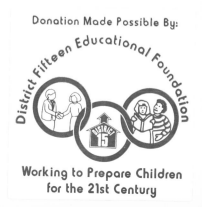

To my dear husband, Glenn, in gratitude for all his
help and encouragement.

The Mystery
at
Haunted Ridge
A Novel

Janna Goodman

Covenant Communications, Inc.

Covenant Communications, Inc.
American Fork, Utah

Printed in the United States of America
First Printing: May 1995

94 95 96 97   10 9 8 7 6 5 4 3 2 1

The Mystery at Haunted Ridge
ISBN 1-55503-694-5

cover illustration by Nathan Pinnock

Chapter 1

TWELVE-YEAR-OLD CARRIE O'BRIEN pulled a comb through her unruly brown hair, then tossed the comb into an open suitcase. She looked around the tiny bedroom that she shared with her sister. In their old house she'd had a room of her own. Now that her family was crowded into a small apartment, she had trouble finding things.

"Heather," she called out, "have you seen my yellow sweater?"

"It's in the bottom of the closet," answered the younger girl.

"Thanks." Carrie picked up her sweater and packed it away. She tucked her Book of Mormon and her journal under its soft, woolen folds.

"Mom said you should have gotten ready last night. Sean did." Heather covered her own short, reddish-gold curls with an Oakland A's baseball cap. She nodded approvingly at her reflection in the mirror. Like Carrie, she was small for her age and had dark, long-lashed eyes and delicate features.

"Sean's a counselor," Carrie said. "He had to leave early."

Heather's pleased expression changed to a pout. "Why can't I come, too?"

"Because you're only six years old. The Golbins are letting the seventh-graders from San Angelo use their campground as an outdoor classroom. If everything works out okay this week, maybe you'll get to go when you're in junior high." Carrie dug several pencils and a notebook out of her backpack and slid them into the side pocket of her suitcase. She held up the fingers of one hand, silently adding up the few things she still needed to find.

Heather folded her arms across her chest and stepped in front of

Carrie. "That's not fair," she said. "I want to see the elves!"

"What makes you think I'll be seeing elves?" Carrie gently moved her sister aside and reached under the bed for an old pair of hiking boots.

"But you said that it's their campground."

Carrie stared at Heather in bewilderment. "What in the world are you talking about?"

"The goblins! Grandma read me a story about them once. She said they're ugly little elves. You told me the goblins are going to let the seventh-graders use their campground."

"Don't be silly, Heather. Goblins aren't real."

"They're not?"

"Of course not! The story that Grandma read to you was just make-believe. The camp belongs to Mr. and Mrs. GOLBIN," Carrie explained, slipping her denim jacket off its hanger. "They're not elves. As far as I know, they're not little, nor ugly, either."

"Oh." Heather frowned.

"Don't look so disappointed. Halloween's less than a month away. Perhaps you'll meet a goblin then."

Mrs. O'Brien stepped into their room. "Carrie," she said, "Amy is on the phone. Don't talk too long. Remember, we need to leave in twenty minutes."

Carrie leaned on her suitcase to snap it closed. She quickly knotted a short length of blue yarn around its handle, then ran into the kitchen to answer the telephone.

"Hi! What's up? Are you ready yet? My parents can give us a ride to school on their way to work."

"I'm not going," her best friend answered. "I woke up with spots this morning."

"Oh, no! Can't you cover them up and go anyway?"

"They're all over me. My mom thinks it's contagious. You could come down with it, too."

"I never get sick." Carrie's eyes narrowed. She couldn't believe the other girl was serious. Was Amy teasing her?

"Are you sure those spots aren't just a new crop of freckles?" she asked suspiciously.

"Carrie! I'm not joking! I don't know what these are, but they're bright pink and they itch. I have to see the doctor tomorrow," Amy said unhappily.

"That's awful!" sympathized Carrie. She wished that there was some way she could make her friend feel better. She had told Amy so much about all the fun she'd had at the Whittier Stake Girls' Camp, that Amy had really been looking forward to their field trip. She glanced down at the short cast that covered her left forearm. Amy had decorated it with colorful, curling lines and squiggles. Carrie traced the designs with her fingers. Suddenly the prospect of spending nearly a week in the Sierra Nevada mountains didn't seem quite so exciting.

"What will I do without you, Amy?" she asked in a small voice. "The only other kids I know at school are the eighth-graders in my Advanced Band class, and none of them are going."

"Your brother and Derek will be there. Sean will take care of you."

Carrie's mouth twisted into a reluctant grin. Amy had an exaggerated opinion of Sean. She thought that he was a genius who could solve any problem.

"Be serious. Sean can't spend all his time worrying about me. He'll be busy. Derek will be, too."

"Why don't you take your trumpet? That would give you something to do. It'll certainly liven up the woods!"

"My folks won't let me. Mom says it would scare the wildlife. Dad's afraid that it might get stolen."

"Sounds like you need something else to keep you busy. How about another mystery to solve?"

Carrie stretched the telephone cord into the living room. She paced back and forth in front of the couch.

"Stop trying to cheer me up," she said. "That's what I ought to be doing for you. You're the one who's sick. Besides, what could be so mysterious about a five-day stay in the forest?"

"Something really weird is going on at that campground. Do you want to hear about it?"

Carrie couldn't resist. "Tell me," she said.

"Some parents volunteered to clean the camp up last August. It needed some work because it hadn't been used in over four years."

"So?"

"You wouldn't believe the strange things that happened while they were there!"

"Like what?"

"Food disappeared, tools vanished, and," Amy lowered her voice to just above a whisper, "one day the drinking water turned dark brown!"

"Oh, yuck! How'd you find out about it?" Carrie was constantly amazed at the way her friend knew everything that went on in their small northern California town.

"Mr. Ohlson was one of the volunteers. He told Greg Spitz, who told his girlfriend, Karen. She told her Aunt Alice May..."

"I get the idea," interrupted Carrie.

"...who's my mom's hairdresser," continued Amy. "And listen to this," she said. "Do you know the name of the place where that camp is located?"

"No."

"Haunted Ridge! It all sounds kind of spooky to me."

Now Carrie's curiosity was REALLY aroused. She thought of Heather's misunderstanding. "Okay," she said. "You win. I'll investigate. Maybe I'll meet some ugly little elves after all."

Chapter 2

"ELVES?" Amy repeated in a puzzled voice.

Carrie grinned. However, before she could explain, her mother called her name. Mrs. O'Brien pointed to her watch, then motioned for Carrie to hang up the phone.

"Listen, Amy," Carrie said in a rush, "we've got to leave in a couple of minutes. I'm sorry about your spots. Hope they don't last long! I'll call you just as soon as I get back home. All right?"

"Wait!" protested Amy. "Explain the elves."

"The goblins?" Carrie's smile broadened. "It was just something my little sister said. I'll tell you all about it later. Bye!"

After hanging up, she poured herself a steaming cup of cocoa from a pan on the stove. She gulped down the hot, sweetened liquid. There wasn't time for cereal, so she grabbed a slice of leftover pepperoni pizza from the refrigerator. She ate it on the way to her bedroom.

Standing on tiptoe, she took a moment to brush the tips of her fingers against the instrument case on the top shelf of her closet. She wished she could have changed her parents' minds, but she'd already lost one trumpet earlier this year. They couldn't afford to buy another one.

Carrie sighed. She picked up her pillow and tucked it under her left arm. She'd already written her name across its embroidered case with a bright blue marker.

Her dad came in as she was struggling to drag her heavy suitcase off the bed. "Let me have that," he ordered. "I'll take it out to the car for you. Your sleeping bag is in the trunk."

"Thanks."

"Are you taking a poncho?" her mother called out. "It might rain."

"What about a jacket?" asked her dad.

"I packed them."

"Good. It gets cold in the mountains this time of year, especially at night." He stopped in the doorway. "Are you all set to go?"

"Almost."

Carrie slipped a cranberry-colored sweatshirt on over her T-shirt. She had to stretch and tug at the left sleeve to force it over her cast. Checking to make sure that Heather was out of sight, she reached behind her dresser mirror. She pulled out a small paper sack and emptied its contents into her pockets. She'd stopped at the corner store yesterday to buy some snacks for the trip. Fortunately her favorite hiding place was still a secret. Her inquisitive younger sister hadn't found it yet.

After family prayer, Carrie silently followed her parents out the front door and down the steps leading to the parking lot. Heather skipped on ahead of them. She liked to be the first one in the car.

Mr. O'Brien ran one hand through hair that had once been as bright as Heather's. He looked intently at his older daughter.

"What's wrong?" he asked as she climbed into their old green Ford.

"Amy's sick. She has to stay home."

"That's a shame, dear," said Mrs. O'Brien. "I hope it's nothing too serious." She stretched her arm back over the seat to pat Carrie's tightly clenched fists. "At least your other friends will be there. You'll still have a good time."

Carrie stared out the window without answering. She didn't know how to tell her mother that she didn't have any other friends her own age.

She had met tall, freckle-faced Amy Noring during the summer. Both girls were in the same grade at school, and both had recently moved into the Chelsea Street Apartments. Amy had a quick wit and a ready smile. She liked to tease, but she never made fun of the difficulty that Carrie had reading and writing.

Carrie had hoped to make new friends in her Young Women's class at church, but she was the only active Beehive in the San Angelo

Second Ward. Sister Yoshito said they needed to fellowship the three other girls. Carrie wondered how she could fellowship someone she'd never even met before. What would she say to them? She felt awkward about telling a total stranger that they ought to come to church. What if they got mad? She thought about the many friends she'd had when her family lived in Whittier. It'd been easy to invite them to the Young Women's activities. She'd known them for so long that she felt comfortable with them. It hadn't mattered much if they laughed at her mistakes. They all knew that she had dyslexia, a learning disability that made it hard for her to read. They liked her anyway.

She leaned her head against the cool, smooth surface of the car window. It shouldn't matter either if the students at her new school laughed, but somehow it did. She closed her eyes.

"Heavenly Father," she prayed silently. "I thank thee for thy son, Jesus Christ, and the beautiful world which He created for us. I'm thankful that Mr. and Mrs. Golbin agreed to let us use their campground. Please bless them." Carrie paused for a moment, trying to sort out her fears and feelings. "Please bless me, too," she added. "I don't know what I'm going to do without Amy. There's got to be someone else here today who needs a friend, too. Help me to find them, I pray, in the name of Jesus Christ, Amen."

Opening her eyes, she glanced over at her sister. Heather had never known a shy day in her entire life. People responded easily and naturally to her. How did she do it?

Carrie sat back and drummed the fingers of her right hand against her leg. "Heather," she said in a low voice, "weren't you scared that no one would like you after we moved?"

"Scared? What do you mean?"

Carrie felt kind of silly asking a six-year-old for advice, but she went ahead anyway. Maybe her sister knew some sort of magic formula.

"Well, tell me how you…"

"Look," interrupted Heather, "we're here! We're at your school."

"Please, Heather," said Mrs. O'Brien, "sit down. As soon as your dad and I help Carrie, we'll take you to school."

Carrie and her parents set her suitcase, pillow, and sleeping bag down next to the other blue-marked items. Beside the pile stood a large, hand-lettered sign.

Her mother read it out loud: "All blue students will board bus number five."

"Goodness!" thought Carrie. "That makes us sound homesick already." She gave her parents a quick hug, then waved goodbye to them as they got back into their car.

"Behave yourself," her father yelled out the window. "Don't get your cast wet!"

Carrie watched them drive away. Maybe she should have taken time to eat a second slice of pizza for breakfast. Her stomach felt strangely hollow inside. She crossed her arms over her chest and leaned against the rough brick wall that bordered the school grounds. As she looked around, she saw that nearly all the other students were clustered together in noisy little groups. No one else stood alone.

"This is ridiculous," she told herself at last. "I feel miserable and it's all my own fault. There's no reason for me to be so nervous about this trip. We won't be in a regular classroom. Nobody will care that I have dyslexia. Nobody will even notice!"

"Yes, they will," nagged a worried little voice deep inside of her. "They'll remember all the dumb things they've seen you do in school. They'll still think you're stupid."

Carrie doubled up her right fist. "Not if I can prove otherwise!" she answered back fiercely. "I'll figure out what's going on at that campground. That will show them I'm not stupid! It will be easy to make friends then."

She took a deep breath. She was tired of being timid and through feeling sorry for herself. It was time to take action.

She waited her turn in line and then stepped resolutely onto bus five. Standing on tip-toe, Carrie tried to see past the students still standing in front of her. Were there any seats left?

She was in luck. Over on the right was a seat with only one occupant: a thin girl with tangled, white-blonde hair. She huddled close to the window as if overwhelmed by all the movement and noise swirling around her.

She glanced in Carrie's direction. Carrie smiled at her and the girl stared back with wide, startled eyes.

Carrie was just about to sit down beside her when she noticed the pair of rowdy boys in the next seat.

Chapter 3

THE TWO BOYS EACH HAD GAP-TOOTHED GRINS, sunburned noses, and ears that stuck out at an angle. Their impish faces looked like mirror images of each other. Obviously they were twins. One of them pointed at the thin girl and snickered. The other one said something under his breath, then they both laughed.

"Oh, no!" thought Carrie. "If I sit there, they'll tease me, too. I've had enough of that!" She quickly turned away.

Three rows down, on the opposite side of the bus, was an empty seat. Carrie hurriedly slipped into it.

"May I sit here, too?" asked a familiar-looking girl. She was small, even shorter than Carrie, and had bleached hair that frizzed around her face like a lop-sided halo.

"I know you," she said, as Carrie silently slid over to make room. "You're Carrie O'Brien from my science class. Remember me? My name is Jillian."

Carrie nodded. "Of course I remember you," she answered. Jillian Vance was difficult to forget. She popped her gum constantly, all the way through their second-period science class.

"I'm surprised you know who I am," said Carrie. "I'm not exactly Ms. Kaufman's star pupil."

"You are awfully quiet in class," acknowledged Jillian.

The corners of Carrie's mouth curved upward in a wry smile. It was true. She tried to draw as little attention to herself as possible during school.

"I guess Ms. Kaufman likes you, though," Jillian continued in a high, breathless voice. "She lets you leave the room whenever we have a test."

Carrie felt her face grow uncomfortably warm. "I can't read very well," she explained, "so I go to the Learning Center to take my tests. An aide reads the questions to me and I write down the answers. I get graded just like everyone else. Honest!"

"Hmmm." Jillian fingered the heart-shaped silver locket that dangled from a chain around her neck. "Sounds easy enough. I wonder if Ms. Kaufman'll let me do that sometime."

Carrie searched for a quick change of subject. She wanted to talk about something a little less embarrassing. As she shifted position, she caught sight of the girl that she'd passed by earlier. The two boys were still bothering her. One of them pulled her hair. The other one giggled.

Carrie nudged Jillian and pointed. "Who's that?"

"The one the Thornberg twins are teasing? That's Megan Zeller."

"Megan Zeller." Carrie repeated the name aloud in a thoughtful voice. She'd heard it before. Sister Yoshito read it each Wednesday night when she called roll in her Young Women's class.

"How can she just sit there? Why doesn't she tell them to leave her alone?" Carrie asked.

Jillian shrugged. "Doesn't have enough sense, I guess."

"So what! That doesn't make it all right for them to torment her like that!"

Jillian stared at Carrie. "Why are you worrying about it? There's nothing you can do."

"Maybe I could have done something," Carrie told herself, "if I hadn't been so afraid that they'd made fun of me as well." She looked again at Megan. The other girl sat hunched over, a curtain of pale hair hiding her face. The twins were taking turns poking her in the back with a pencil. Carrie felt a little sick inside.

"Megan is a total loser," said the girl sitting directly in front of Carrie. "If you're smart, you'll stay away from her." She spoke without turning her head. All Carrie could see of her was shiny black hair pulled back into a sleek ponytail.

"Well," thought Carrie ruefully, "being smart isn't something I've ever been accused of before." She jumped to her feet. "Excuse me," she said, "I made a mistake. I sat in the wrong seat."

"What?" Jillian's gum nearly fell out of her mouth.

"It's nothing personal," Carrie hastened to assure her. "I just have to move. There's something I need to take care of right away." She squeezed past Jillian and crossed the aisle to sit beside Megan. She turned to face the twins.

"Don't tease her anymore," she whispered. "Please."

One of them grinned broadly at Carrie and leaned forward. He poked Megan again, then passed the pencil to his brother.

"IF YOU DO THAT ONE MORE TIME, I'M GOING TO TELL THE DRIVER!" Carrie said in a loud, clear voice that could be heard the length of the bus.

Everyone stopped talking. It was completely quiet as the bus driver, a grim-faced woman in her fifties, slowly walked down the aisle. She stopped in front of the boys.

"Is there a problem here?" she asked, glaring at them.

They both shoved their hands behind their backs and vigorously shook their heads.

"Good," she said sternly. "I don't allow trouble on my bus."

As soon as she moved away, the boy on the left stuck his tongue out at Carrie. "Tattletale," growled the one on the right.

Carrie slumped in her seat. They hadn't even left the school grounds and already she'd managed to make at least three people mad at her. Things certainly weren't going the way she'd planned!

The driver turned the key in the ignition. One by one, the buses drove out of the parking lot. They followed the main highway out of town and across the Feather River. They passed dairy farms and rice fields ready for harvest. Soon the road began to twist and turn as it wound through the brown, dry foothills. The air smelled different now—dusty, like a pile of fresh-fallen leaves.

Carrie tried, with little success, to start a conversation with Megan. No matter what she said, the other girl replied as briefly and reluctantly as possible. It was plain she didn't want to talk.

After a while, the boys behind them started kicking their seat. Carrie gritted her teeth. If she didn't put a stop to that soon, the rest of the ride would really be miserable!

She pulled four king-size chocolate bars out of the front pocket of her sweatshirt. She tossed one into Megan's lap, set another aside for herself, then turned around. She held up the two remaining pieces of candy.

"This is a peace offering," she said. "I'd like to end hostilities. Tell me your names."

One of the boys tried to snatch the candy. She moved it just out of his reach.

"I'm Kevin," said his brother. "He's Evan."

"My name is Carrie. If you leave Megan and me alone, I'll give you one Hershey's Bar now and another one when we arrive at camp. Is it a deal?"

"Deal!" they shouted in unison.

The boys quit annoying them after that. Carrie bent forward with her elbows on her knees and her chin resting on her hands. Her mind was still filled with unanswered questions. She kept thinking about what Amy had said. What had been going on at the campground? Was it just a series of harmless pranks, or something more serious? And why was the place called Haunted Ridge? Could there really be a mystery she could solve? She twisted a lock of hair around her finger. Maybe some of the other students had heard about the strange happenings. Perhaps she could ask Jillian about it later. "That is," she thought glumly, "if Jillian will ever speak to me again."

Carrie tore her candy wrapper open with her teeth. As she nibbled on the sweet-tasting chocolate, she looked around. Everyone on the bus seemed excited about the trip. Everyone, that is except Megan. Carrie stopped chewing and studied her seat mate.

Megan hadn't eaten her candy. Instead, she gripped it so hard that milk chocolate oozed through a hole in the wrapper and seeped between her rigidly curled fingers. She stared straight ahead without seeming to notice the gooey mess. Every few seconds a shudder racked her thin body.

"Good grief!" thought Carrie with a sense of shock. "What's wrong with her? She looks scared half to death!"

Chapter 4

CARRIE SETTLED BACK against her seat. She frowned in puzzlement. Did the other girl know something about the camp that the rest of them didn't? If only Megan was more talkative!

The road curved upward, past Grizzly Lake Dam. They drove through hills dotted with scrub oak and granite boulders, then into pine-topped mountains. Several logging trucks, going the opposite direction, roared by them. Eventually the buses turned off the highway onto a rough, narrow road. The pavement was cracked and patched. It led them deep into the dark green woods. They passed pine and fir trees planted close together in straight rows.

There was a sign. Kevin read it out loud: "Christmas trees for sale, next right."

"I wonder if they sell the decorations, too," mused Evan.

"I doubt it," Carrie answered.

"We should reach camp soon," she heard someone in the back say.

"I certainly hope so," she muttered under her breath. She wasn't sure whether she felt excited, or just plain nervous. Either way, she was anxious for the bumpy ride to end. Some of the other students were beginning to look a little car-sick.

Evan leaned over her shoulder and jabbed her cast with his forefinger.

"What did you do to your arm?" asked Kevin.

"I broke my wrist."

"Does it hurt?" inquired Evan.

"Not any more."

"How'd you break it?" Kevin asked curiously.

"I fell down some stairs."

Evan snorted. "That was clumsy!"

"I was pretty scared at the time," admitted Carrie. "I thought I'd seen a ghost." She didn't tell the twins that it had happened while she was helping her neighbors hunt for a long-lost treasure. She didn't know if they would believe her anyway. Yet, somehow, the memory gave her both comfort and courage. *I solved a mystery once before,* she told herself. *I can do it again!*

"Was it a real ghost?" asked Kevin.

Carrie shook her head.

"Have you ever met a real, live witch?" he asked. "We know where one lives."

Evan pointed out the window.

"See that house?" asked Kevin. "It belongs to a witch. Our Pop said so."

In the distance, Carrie glimpsed a wooden building. Its sagging roof and broken porch were barely visible through the trees.

"That old shack?"

"No," answered Evan impatiently. "The OTHER one."

Carrie looked again. Past the battered cabin, she could see a cheery, yellow-painted house nestled snugly beside a small orchard. It was decorated with delicate white trim and an old-fashioned weather vane that spun gently in the breeze. She couldn't imagine anything looking less like a witch's house.

"Are you sure that's what your dad said?"

"Positive," Kevin assured her. "He and Mom met her when they came in August to clean up the campground. Pop called her the witch of Haunted Ridge."

Evan agreed.

Before she could question the boys further, the bus veered sharply to the right. Carrie was caught off balance. She had to hang on the seat in front of her to keep from sliding into Megan.

The bus bounced along a rock-strewn dirt road for a few moments, then lurched to a stop. Two friendly-looking men stood in the road, blocking their way. One of them wore a bright yellow bandanna knotted around his neck. He tipped his hat to the students as he greeted them. His bearded companion had such a jolly, round, and ruddy face, that Carrie was reminded of a Christmas elf. *All he needs,* she thought, *is a sprig of holly in his hair.*

"Are we here?"

"Where are the cabins?"

"Hey! It's wet out there!"

Carrie listened to the voices clamoring around her. "Why are we stopping?" she wondered out loud. "Aren't we supposed to drive all the way into camp?"

"Excuse me," she said to Megan. She leaned across the other girl to get a better view. "Oh, my," she whispered, blinking in surprise, "what a mess!" The meadow was filled with mud, water, and debris from the nearby creek. Now she understood why the buses hadn't gone any farther.

Their driver shut off the engine and slowly rose to her feet. She motioned for silence.

"The ground is too wet for these heavy vehicles to cross," she said. "You will have to walk the rest of the way."

Immediately the air was filled with groans and protests.

"Stop complaining and get moving," she ordered. "Don't forget your luggage. I don't want to take it back to San Angelo with me."

Carrie slipped off her shoes and socks and rolled up her pants. Following the other students, she stepped gingerly off the bus and onto the soggy grass.

"Ooooooh," moaned Jillian, "it feels disgusting!" She peered nervously at the weeds growing near their feet. "Are there any bugs around here? I hate bugs!"

"The ground is kind of squishy," Carrie agreed cautiously, "but I haven't seen any insects yet."

Jillian blew a large bubble and let it pop.

"I hope you're not still mad at me," Carrie said in a rush. "I didn't mean to be rude. I just couldn't stand to watch those boys..."

"You just wanted to sit by that loser," interrupted a harsh voice. "I warned you to stay away from her," said the girl who had sat in front of them on the bus.

Carrie stiffened. She hated to have anyone, especially someone her own age, boss her around.

"Who are you?" she demanded.

"Raven. Raven Blake. Next time do as you're told!"

Carrie stared straight into the other girl's light hazel eyes. With her sharp features, and hair that was as black and glossy as a crow's wing, the name Raven suited the girl. Carrie would have found that amusing if she hadn't been struggling to keep her temper.

"Forget it," said Jillian. She tugged on Raven's arm. "Let's go."

The two girls waded over to pick up their belongings. Carrie remained where she was. It had suddenly occurred to her that she was going to have a great deal of trouble getting her things into camp.

"Where's the rest of our candy?"

"Yeah, you promised!"

Carrie dug two more chocolate bars out of her pocket. The Thornberg twins grabbed them out of her hand and ran off.

"Darn!" she said. "I should have asked them to help me before I gave them the candy."

A pair of dogs howled in the distance. Their mournful cries blended together in an eerie duet. The sound came from the west. "The poor things must be chained up somewhere down the road," thought Carrie. She wondered if Sean heard the animals, too. He'd had to give away his little terrier, Toby, when they had moved to San Angelo. Carrie knew it was one of the hardest things he'd ever had to do. Why couldn't they have rented an apartment that allowed pets? For a moment she felt as down-hearted as the dogs. She shook her head to clear her thoughts. Grumbling to herself wasn't going to do any good.

"Need a hand?" asked Derek Graham.

She looked up in surprise to see her older brother's outspoken best friend. "Oh! Thanks," she said. "I don't know if I can manage by myself. My cast is sure to get in the way." She located her luggage, then asked, "Where's Sean?"

"Helping Mrs. Delgado. He sent me to find you." Derek effortlessly lifted Carrie's heavy suitcase, then hefted her sleeping bag onto his broad shoulders. "Think you can handle your pillow?"

"Of course! I'm not helpless." Grateful as she was for Derek's aid, Carrie was not entirely pleased about having to accept it. When the two of them had first met, he'd accused her of being a thief and she had heartily disliked him. She still didn't feel completely at ease with him, but she was glad they weren't enemies anymore. Like the O'Brien family, sixteen-year-old Derek and his parents belonged to the Church of Jesus Christ of Latter-day Saints.

Carrie and Derek made slow, careful progress across the meadow. The muddy grass under their feet was slick and they had to watch their step. Some of the students tried to hurry. They skidded over the ground, arms and legs flailing in all directions. Several fell into the wild blackberry bushes that grew in masses along the creek bank. Carrie heard them yelp in painful dismay as they landed in the brambles. She was glad she'd taken off her shoes.

The two jovial men who had greeted the bus were nowhere in sight. When she questioned Derek, he told her that they were businessmen who lived nearby.

"Businessmen? In the middle of the woods?"

"They sell Christmas trees," Derek explained.

"Really? I should have guessed. As soon as I saw them, I thought of the holidays. One of them looks just like one of Santa's helpers."

Derek shrugged. A lock of dark hair fell in his eyes and he brushed it aside. Carrie had the impression that his mind was on something else.

"What happened here?" she asked when they finally reached the bridge. "Did the creek overflow?"

"You guessed it. There's a log dam upstream. It broke last night. We spent a good part of the morning rebuilding it." Derek flexed the muscles in his upper arms as if they were still a bit sore. "What a job that was!"

"How'd the dam break?"

Derek's deep blue eyes looked troubled. "I don't know," he said. "It was supposed to be sturdy enough. Mrs. Delgado told us it'd been there for a long time. Hey!" He stopped so suddenly that Carrie nearly stumbled into him. "You're not thinking about playing detective, are you?"

"Maybe."

"Don't! There's something odd about this place. I don't know what it is, but it gives me the creeps!"

"Nobody asked you to worry about me," she said, irritation edging her voice.

"Well, somebody should," muttered Derek. He followed her across the wooden bridge and down the narrow, dusty road into the main part of camp.

They had just reached the kitchen area when a terrified scream echoed through the pines.

"There's blood coming out of the faucet!" someone yelled.

Chapter 5

CARRIE TUCKED HER PILLOW UNDER ONE ARM and sprinted toward the noise. Most of the students had already gathered in front of a two-story timber and stone building. She pushed her way through them until she came face-to-face with Sean, her fifteen-year-old brother.

A huge grin spread over his face. "I knew curiosity would bring you running," he said. "Where's Derek?"

"He's around here someplace. What's going on?"

"I'm right behind you," snapped Derek. He dropped Carrie's things at her feet. "You could have waited for me."

She ignored him. "Please, Sean, tell me what happened."

Her brother ran one hand through his thick, dark-red hair. "Heidi Jacobs turned on the water, then went into hysterics. That's her over there," he said, pointing towards a sobbing seventh-grader, "talking to the camp director."

Carrie peered over his shoulder. She could see Heidi leaning against a plump, motherly-looking woman.

"It was red," the girl was saying in between hiccoughs, "just like b-b-blood, and it splashed all over me!"

"Yes, I see," said the woman. She reached over and turned the handle. The water that spilled out of the faucet ran first pink, then crystal clear.

"I'm told there was a similar problem over the summer," she said, "but when the well was tested, it proved not to be contaminated. Apparently someone poured a harmless vegetable dye down the pipe. It was nothing more than a foolish prank."

"I don't care," gulped Heidi. "I'm not drinking that water!"

Murmurs of "Me neither," "No way!" and "Not me," rippled through the crowd in response. Carrie didn't blame them. She wasn't anxious for a taste-test either.

"You won't have to drink it," answered the director, her voice still patient. "We'll use the water from the kitchen, instead. It's on a separate well system."

Carrie watched with growing respect as the woman soothed Heidi, calmed the students, then welcomed them all to the Golbin's Campground.

"Who is she?" asked Carrie, "and how in the world did she get everyone quieted down so quickly?"

"That's Mrs. Delgado," answered Sean. "She has a knack for getting people to do what she wants."

"I'll say!" Derek said, obviously remembering the dam. "I can't believe we were up here at daybreak, hauling logs!"

Carrie scuffed the toe of her right shoe into the rust-colored earth. "Amy told me something funny was going on around here. A few minutes ago, Derek said pretty much the same thing."

Derek shook the hair out of his eyes with an impatient toss of his head. Carrie recognized the gesture. It meant he was annoyed.

"I think they're both right," Sean said.

Carrie's spirits perked up immediately. If her brother was interested in the mystery, he would help her solve it.

"We've got to talk," she said.

"Okay. Meet Derek and me after dinner at the big rock behind the lodge."

Derek groaned. "You're not going to encourage her, are you?"

"Why not? She's good at figuring things out. Goodness knows we could use the help." Sean rubbed the back of his neck and his expression grew serious. "One thing after another has fallen apart since we got here," he said.

"You haven't heard the worst of it," said an attractive black girl with smooth, clear skin and the lithe body of a dancer. She stepped out of the crowd to stand beside Derek.

"Hi, Tia," said Sean, "What's gone wrong now?"

"Apparently the cabin assignment list disappeared while we were fixing the dam. We can't find it anywhere. It's going to be total chaos trying to organize these twelve-year-olds without it!"

Carrie's eyes widened. "Another prank?"

Tia threw her hands in the air. "Who knows? Maybe a squirrel ate it." She flung her long, beaded braids over her shoulder. "What a way to start the week!"

"That's for sure!" Sean turned to his sister. "By the way, I don't see Amy. Usually you two are never far apart. Did she come on a different bus?"

Carrie explained about the spots.

Sean sympathized with her over Amy's ailment, then said goodbye. He ambled over to the kitchen area where the rest of the counselors were gathering.

Mrs. Delgado and the teachers began separating the students into groups of five and then herding them toward the counselors. Carrie chuckled when she noticed Evan and Kevin heading for Derek. He wasn't the most even-tempered person she had ever met, and those two boys reminded her of a pair of poorly-trained puppies. She knew he'd have his hands full with them.

All at once Carrie realized that she didn't have any idea who was going to room with her. Would anyone want to?

"You can be with us," said Jillian, as if she'd guessed what Carrie had been thinking. "Raven said so."

Carrie's spirits rose immediately. She felt even better when she saw Tia Hamilton walk in their direction. Tia was the Laurel class president in their ward. She also shared a computer class with Sean and he spoke highly of her.

With Tia was a tall girl with her nose in a book. Her golden brown hair fell in heavy waves past her waist. Peering over the top of her glasses, she gave the others a vague smile.

"That's Beth Astin," Jillian whispered in Carrie's ear. "She reads ALL the time."

Tia surveyed the little group standing before her. "We're one short," she said. "There are supposed to be five of you."

"Four is fine," said Raven evenly. "We don't want anyone else."

"Yes, we do. Isn't there someone else you'd like to ask to join us?"

Raven shook her head. Jillian did the same. Beth sat down on a rock with her book. She continued reading.

Carrie knew what she had to do. She searched until she spotted Megan, standing in the shadows beneath a hemlock tree at the edge of the clearing. Megan's head drooped so that her pale hair shaded her face, just as it had on the bus. Carrie remembered how lonely she'd felt earlier. Megan must be feeling that same way now.

Carrie ran over and grabbed her by the hand. "We need you to be in our group," she said as she pulled the reluctant girl forward.

"There are five of us now," Carrie said. She stared defiantly at Raven.

Raven's face froze into a still, cold mask.

Chapter 6

"LISTEN TO ME CAREFULLY," Raven said in a silky voice, as she and Carrie dragged their suitcases toward their quarters. "Megan can stay on one condition. I want you to do me a favor."

Carrie raised her eyebrows. Since when was Raven in charge?

"It's only a little thing," coaxed the other girl. A smile softened her sharp features. "Say you'll do it."

"How little?" Carrie asked guardedly.

"Just introduce me to Derek Graham later today. Don't tell me you don't know him. I saw the two of you talking together."

Carrie's jaw dropped. "You want to meet Derek? Why?"

Raven rolled her eyes. "What's the matter with you? Haven't you noticed? He's the best-looking boy in the entire camp!"

Carrie was amazed. Imagine Raven thinking she had some sort of influence over Derek! She struggled to keep a straight face. She sensed that Raven wouldn't appreciate it if she burst out laughing.

"Sure," she replied. "I can introduce you to Derek. That's easy enough. I'll have to warn you though, Derek has an independent mind. He'll decide for himself whether or not he wants to get to know you better."

"Tell him we're friends. You do want to be friends, don't you?"

Carrie decided she must have misjudged Raven. "I'd like that," she said eagerly. "We'll talk to Derek together after dinner tonight. That's a promise!"

Raven favored Carrie with a brief, satisfied nod. She stopped in front of the cabin that Tia had just entered. She glanced up at the sign above the door.

"Song Sparrows," she read aloud. She cocked her head to one side and considered the name. "That doesn't sound too bad. We can take this one."

Carrie grinned. "It could have been worse," she agreed. "I'd hate to be called skunks, or something else equally awful." Actually, she was pleased. She rather liked the name of the cabin that their counselor had chosen for them. She followed Raven inside.

Tia asked everyone to introduce themselves. She wrote their names down on her note pad.

Carrie had to endure another round of questions about her cast. When the others finally tired of the subject, she looked around. The cabin was not only little, it was sparsely furnished. A shiny, metal-framed mirror was its sole decoration. There was one tiny window on the far wall, but most of the light came from a single, unshaded bulb that hung from the ceiling.

"Where do we set our gear?" she asked Tia.

"Just find an empty bunk. There are storage cupboards at the foot of each bed."

To Carrie's astonishment, she discovered that her sleeping bag and pillow were already neatly laid out on one of the three top bunks. That was terrific! Now she wouldn't have to make a second trip to the clearing. She looked at Tia.

Tia shook her head in response to Carrie's unspoken question. "I didn't bring them in," she said.

"Then who did?"

Without speaking, Raven pulled Carrie's things off the bed and dumped them on the lower bunk. She put her own in their place.

"You're short," Jillian explained to Carrie. "You have to take the bottom bed so Raven won't bump her head."

Carrie's brows drew together in a frown, but she decided it wasn't worth arguing about.

Beth looked up from the stack of paperback novels she was sorting. "Megan brought in your bedding," she said.

"Really? Thanks, Megan!" Carrie was amazed. The other girl had seemed too wrapped up in her own misery to notice anyone else's difficulties.

Megan gave Carrie a small, hesitant smile. She sat cross-legged in the corner, struggling to untie the cords that bound her battered suitcase. Carrie knelt down beside her to help.

"My grandfather loaned it to me," Megan said shyly. "The latch broke ages ago."

"Have you taken a good look at mine? It's definitely seen better days." Carrie chuckled. "Just think of them as antiques."

At last the knots in the rope slipped through their fingers. Immediately the case flopped open. Crimson and purple scarves, a chain of interlocking silver rings, and half a dozen decks of brilliantly-colored cards spilled out onto the rough plank floor.

Carrie blinked. "Wow!" she exclaimed. "What kind of camping equipment is that?"

Megan's face flushed a dull red. "I've never been camping before," she admitted. "I didn't know what to bring."

"But..."

"Better get moving," interrupted Tia. "We meet for our first class soon. I don't want the Song Sparrows to be late."

Carrie rose to her feet. She unlatched her own suitcase and began putting away her things. There were questions she was just dying to ask Megan, but she wasn't sure where to start. She'd never met anyone before who was so timid. She looked over her shoulder as she straightened out her sleeping bag. Raven stood next to Megan, talking to her in a low voice. Carrie couldn't hear what they were saying. She thought Raven must be trying to make friends. That was a good sign.

A minute later, Raven climbed up onto her bed. "Megan! Get me something to read," she commanded.

Megan ran to the cupboard and grabbed a magazine from the top shelf. She gave it to Raven.

"Not that one, stupid! Get me this month's issue."

Carrie stiffened. What was going on between those two? She glanced at the other girls to see if they knew. Jillian turned away, as if embarrassed. Beth wasn't listening.

"And while you're up," continued Raven, "take care of my clothes."

Megan got the other magazine, then reached for the cases that Raven had dropped on the ground.

Carrie started to protest, but their counselor beat her to it.

"Megan, you don't have to fetch and carry for Raven," Tia said. Exasperation sharpened her voice.

"I don't mind," Megan said miserably. Her fingers trembled as she slipped Raven's sheepskin jacket onto a hanger.

Carrie burst out, "Well, you should mind! Let Raven do her own chores."

Megan's wide, gray eyes filled with tears. "Leave me alone, Carrie," she whispered.

Carrie walked out the door. She brushed some pine needles off a flat rock and sat down. Wrapping her arms around her legs, she rocked back and forth. She wasn't mad at Megan. She just wished the other girl knew how to stand up for herself.

Their counselor wasn't ready to let the subject drop. Carrie heard her say, "Raven, since Megan is taking care of your clothes, it's only fair that you do the same for her. Her clothing needs to be put away, too."

"Why should I? You heard Megan. She doesn't mind helping me," Raven replied in an insolent voice.

Carrie turned her head and peered through the open doorway.

"Just do it!" Tia placed her hands on her hips. She tapped her foot impatiently on the floor, waiting for Raven to comply.

Raven's mouth thinned into an angry line. Wordlessly she slid off her bed. She stomped over to Megan's open suitcase. She picked out a pair of worn corduroy pants, held them up high, and inspected them with insulting slowness.

"Oh, Megan," she drawled, "these are too fine for camping. Why didn't you bring some old clothes?"

Jillian giggled nervously.

"Quiet!" snapped Tia.

Raven tossed the pants into the bottom of the storage cabinet. She dangled a threadbare sweater from the tips of her fingers, holding it as far away from her nose as possible.

Jillian laughed again, louder this time. Beth frowned at the noise, but she was too deep in her book to pay much attention to it.

Carrie doubled up her fists. Even though Megan didn't want her to interfere, she couldn't bear to watch this any longer. There had to be a way she could end the teasing without offending Raven!

Chapter 7

CARRIE FOLDED HER ARMS. She bent her head for a moment in prayer, then called out, "Hey, Raven, want some help?" She jumped up and ran back inside. "You hand me the clothes and I'll take care of them for you." Carrie snatched a faded, long-sleeved shirt from Raven's hands. "Come on," she urged. "It'll go faster if we work together."

Raven acted surprised by Carrie's offer, but she didn't complain. Tia looked relieved as the tension in the little cabin eased. There was no more mockery as the girls folded and put away the rest of their things.

"That's it," said Raven. "We're through." She kicked the empty case aside.

Carrie wondered what had happened to the colorful scarves, cards, and silver rings. They seemed to have vanished. She lay down on her bed and drummed her fingers against its metal frame. That strange assortment of things reminded her of something she'd seen before. What was it? She hesitated to ask Megan while the others were listening. They might start tormenting Megan again. It'd be best to talk to her later.

A loud, clanging sound disrupted Carrie's thoughts. She got up and peeped out the door. An old-fashioned school bell hung from the branch of a Douglas fir. Mrs. Delgado was ringing it vigorously.

Tia consulted her notes. "It's eleven o'clock. Time for the Animal Adaptation class. Don't forget your pencils and paper." She pried the book out of Beth's fingers and shepherded the girls outside.

The sun had climbed higher in the sky. The day was warming up.

Carrie noticed that their surroundings were a little different from the mountains in Southern California where she'd gone to an LDS girls' camp. The forest growth was a deeper green. The trees seemed to be taller and the underbrush was thicker.

The area around their sleeping quarters had been raked free of brush. Beyond that, madrone leaves, pine cones, and the long needles from ponderosa and sugar pines covered the ground. The pine cones crunched under their feet as they walked. Across the clearing she saw the boys milling around in front of their cabins. Carrie looked for Sean. Usually he was easy to find—his red hair stood out like a flame. At last she spotted him wiping the rectangular tables that were set up next to the kitchen.

Carrie sniffed the clean, fresh air. "I hope we eat lunch soon," she said.

"My grandpa said he always gets a big appetite in the mountains," Megan responded in a shy voice.

Carrie grinned. "I'm hungry all the time, no matter where I am." They followed Tia as she led the way to the lodge. Folding chairs were arranged in rows beside the timber and stone building.

"This is Mr. Lee," Tia said, introducing a slender man with thick, horn-rimmed glasses. "He teaches biology at the high school."

Mr. Lee waited until they were joined by five other groups of students. When they were all seated, he shuffled the sheaf of papers resting on his makeshift podium.

"I expect all of you to take notes," he announced, looking at them through his spectacles. "There will be no exceptions, no excuses."

Carrie bit her lip so hard it hurt. Any kind of writing assignment made her nervous. She knew perfectly well that she couldn't form words fast enough to take proper notes. Without thinking, she pressed her pencil down too hard. The lead broke just as Mr. Lee began his lecture.

She stared at her paper in dismay. Now what? "I'd better listen closely," she thought, "then maybe I won't get into trouble." She concentrated on Mr. Lee's words and the enlarged photographs that he displayed. Soon she became interested in his description of the gray squirrel and how it adapted to forest living. She even had to smother a giggle when he described the squirrels using their long, fluffy tails to protect themselves from dive-bombing woodpeckers.

Class ended when Mrs. Delgado rang the bell at twelve o'clock. Carrie was delighted to discover that this was the signal for lunch. On her way back down the trail, she felt a tug on the hood of her sweatshirt. She whirled around and looked into the mischievous faces of Evan Thornberg and his brother, Kevin.

"Hello," said Kevin. "How about another candy bar?"

"You've got to be kidding, Kevin," she answered. "You guys already ate nearly all my snacks."

Evan reached for Megan, who was right behind Carrie. "I'll bet she's got some," he said, smacking his lips.

Megan shrank back in fear.

"Evan!" Carrie exclaimed. "No more handouts! Go away if you can't behave yourself."

"We were just trying to be friendly," Kevin said in a wounded voice.

"There you are!" Derek clapped a firm hand on a shoulder of each twin. "I was looking for you," he said through gritted teeth. "Quit bothering the girls. It's mealtime."

"We weren't bothering them," protested Kevin. "We like to talk to Carrie."

"SHE can tell us apart," added Evan, his green eyes alight with glee.

Derek gave the boys a gentle shove in the direction of the food. "Go eat," he said. He turned to Carrie. "Can you really tell those two imps apart?" he asked.

"Sure, can't you?"

Derek brushed the hair back from his forehead. "No, and I'm going out of my mind trying to keep track of them," he blurted out. "They're never where they're supposed to be, and neither one can stand, sit, or even lie still."

"Why don't you separate them? Put Evan in another cabin."

"Because the other counselors don't want either him or Kevin. Nobody will trade with me."

"What about Sean? Is he having as much trouble with his group?"

"He doesn't have a group. Mrs. Delgado found out that he's a year younger than the rest of us. He runs errands for her instead." Derek shoved both hands into the pockets of his blue jeans. His straight, black brows drew together in a scowl. "Sean ought to have this job," he said gruffly. "He could handle it."

Carrie silently agreed. Her good-natured brother got along well with everybody. He was not only smart, he was patient.

"Do you know what the worst part is?" asked Derek.

Carrie shook her head.

"I can't tell which twin I'm speaking to when I yell at them. How do you do it?"

"It's easy," she said.

"Hey, Derek!" someone shouted. "Better get over here. There's a couple of kids emptying the salt and pepper packets at your table."

Derek groaned. He sprinted toward the kitchen.

"I'll tell you later," Carrie called out after him. "Poor Derek," she said to Megan. "Kevin and Evan seem to be giving him a bad time."

Megan shuddered. "How can you stand those two boys?" she whispered. "They're horrible!"

"They remind me of my six-year-old cousin, Ritchie. He drives everyone crazy, but he's really not such a bad kid. You just have to get used to him."

Carrie found where the rest of her cabin mates were sitting. She and Megan joined them. On the table was a platter stacked high with chicken sandwiches, a gallon jug of ice-cold milk, bowls filled with tortilla chips and a basket full of fresh fruit. Carrie grabbed two sandwiches, then bit into a tart, juicy pippin apple.

As they ate, Raven entertained them by telling jokes and funny stories about the people sitting around them. Even Megan managed a faint smile when Raven related a humorous incident involving Kevin, Evan, and a near-sighted math teacher. Carrie was amused almost in spite of herself. Raven had a way with words.

Carrie had finished a handful of chips and was on her second glass of milk when she noticed how much the temperature had risen. Now that the sun was directly overhead, all the coolness of the morning had evaporated. It was too warm to be wearing cold-weather clothing.

Carrie got up from the table. "I'll be back in a minute," she told Tia. "I need to put away my sweatshirt." She took a few steps, then stopped. She was unsure which cabin was theirs. They all looked alike.

"Remember," said Tia helpfully, "we're the Song Sparrows. Just look for the sign above the door."

Carrie felt her face redden. It would take forever for her to sound out the name above every single door! She gulped.

"Uh, what if I have trouble seeing the sign? How do I find the right one?" she asked.

Raven looked at her thoughtfully, as if processing a particularly interesting piece of information.

"It's seventh from the end," said Tia. "Just count and you'll find it."

"Thanks," said Carrie. She turned and fled toward the cabins.

Eventually she located their cabin. She slipped off her sweatshirt, easing it carefully over her cast, and opened the door.

It was dark inside. Hardly any sunshine made it through the tiny, tree-shaded window. As she entered, she stumbled over something soft and damp. What was that on the ground? Her eyes hadn't had time to adjust to the dark. Everything looked dim and indistinct. She put one hand on the middle bunk to steady herself, then quickly withdrew it. The bedpost was wet! Carrie drew her breath in sharply, but inhaling made her cough so hard she nearly gagged. The air was heavy with the cloying smell of hair spray and perfume. If only she could see better! Something was wrong. She was sure of it! Finally her searching fingers found the string that turned on the light. She pulled it.

Carrie was so shocked at what the light revealed that her knees buckled. She sat down with a thump on the floor.

Chapter 8

THE CABIN WAS IN SHAMBLES. A pillow lay on the floor, soaked with a clear, citrus-scented liquid. Books were scattered from one end of the room to the other. The contents of Raven's cupboard were scattered in all directions. Her sleeping bag was soggy. Megan's blankets had been bundled into a pile. Jillian's bed was heaped with clothes and so was Tia's.

Carrie rubbed her forehead with stiff fingers. The place looked as if it had been decorated by a poltergeist. She rose to her feet and started picking up paperbacks.

"Just what do you think you're doing?"

Carrie spun around. The cold fury in Raven's face chilled her.

"Trying to straighten up," she replied. "Somebody trashed our cabin."

The others crowded through the door.

"My books!" cried Beth. "What have you done to my books?"

"Nothing!" Carrie answered indignantly.

Jillian burst into tears.

Tia put a comforting arm around her. "Everything can be cleaned," she said. "We'll all work together."

"What about my perfume?" wailed Jillian. "That bottle was almost full. Now it's all gone!"

"Stop bawling," snarled Raven. "You shouldn't have brought it." She picked her pillow up and wrinkled her nose. "I can't sleep on this!" she yelled. She hurled the pillow across the room.

Megan slipped past Raven and retreated to the far corner. She didn't say anything, but Carrie could tell she was frightened. All the color seemed to have drained out of her face.

Tia's warm brown eyes looked troubled. "I wish I knew who was responsible for this," she said. "I don't understand how it could have happened. We all ate together."

"One of us left early," commented Beth. As she gathered her books together, she kept glancing suspiciously at Carrie.

"That's right," agreed Jillian, "and look," she added in a high, accusing voice. "There's nothing wrong with any of Carrie's belongings. Not even her toothbrush is out of place! Everyone else's stuff has been thrown all over the cabin."

"Hey, wait a moment!" Carrie protested. "All I did was come in here to drop off my sweatshirt." She surveyed the room and her heart sank. It was true. Her possessions were the only things left untouched.

Megan buried her face in one of her blankets. "Carrie d-d-didn't do it," she said in a muffled voice. "It m-m-must have been somebody else."

"Who?" demanded Raven.

Megan cringed. She didn't answer.

Carrie marvelled at Megan's courage. She hadn't expected Megan to have enough nerve to stick up for someone else.

"Megan has a point. This really isn't Carrie's style," Tia said firmly. She flipped her long braids over her shoulder. "It could have been done by students from a different cabin. I'll ask the other counselors about it. Maybe they saw something."

"Thanks," Carrie said. It wasn't the first time she'd had reason to be grateful her brother was so well liked. People who knew Sean generally assumed that she was a decent person, as well.

"But I want to know who dumped out my perfume," wailed Jillian.

"Let Carrie figure it out," Raven snapped.

"What?" asked Beth. She squinted at Carrie over the top of her glasses.

"Oh, didn't you know? She's a great detective," Raven informed them all. "She's going to solve our mystery for us."

Carrie's face burned with embarrassment. Raven must have overheard her conversation in the meadow with Derek. How she wished she'd kept quiet!

Tia threw her hands up in exasperation. "Enough talk," she said. "Let's get moving." She checked her watch. "We have twenty minutes of free time left before the next class. If we rush, we should make it." She put both hands on her hips and gave directions to each girl. "Jillian, you and I will clear off our beds. Raven, put everything back in your storage cabinent. Beth, when you're though taking care of those books, give Raven a hand. Carrie, help Megan with her blankets. After that, I want you two to take Raven's pillow and sleeping bag behind the kitchen. There's a hose and clothesline there. Wash down the bedding thoroughly and hang it out to dry. When you're finished, meet the rest of us at the lodge."

Within moments, the cabin was a beehive of activity. Carrie and Megan quickly completed their first task, then headed for the next.

"Here," Megan said softly, "you take the pillow. I can manage the sleeping bag."

"All right." Carrie motioned for Megan to lead the way. As they trudged down the leaf-strewn path, Carrie turned Raven's words over and over in her mind. The campground mystery had suddenly become a very personal matter. She no longer cared if she impressed the others. She just wanted them to trust her again.

They followed the trail to the rear of the kitchen. Megan pinned the sleeping bag and pillow to the clothesline. Carrie directed a steady stream of water on the bedding. Fortunately, the hair spray rinsed off easily enough. The fragrance was a different matter.

"It still smells like rancid lemonade, doesn't it?" she asked.

Megan ducked her head. "I don't think it'll wash out," she murmured. "Raven's going to be angry."

"Maybe there are extra pillows in the lodge. At least we can hope her sleeping bag dries before bedtime." Carrie shut off the faucet. "Megan," she began hesitantly, "why does this place scare you so much? What's going on here?"

Megan's head jerked up. She stared at Carrie with huge, frightened eyes.

"Don't ask," she whispered. "It's dangerous."

"Do you know how it got the name Haunted Ridge?"

Before Megan could answer, the sound of the school bell pealed through the forest. Carrie glanced in its direction. She knew they'd better hurry. Their second class was about to start. When she turned back, Megan was nowhere in sight. She'd vanished as silently and secretly as a ghost.

Carrie jogged back alone to meet their cabin mates. She crossed the clearing at a run, dodging the few students still roaming around.

"Slow down!" her brother called out. He leaned against a post in front of the lodge. "Don't you ever just walk anywhere?"

She grinned. "Not if I can help it." She knew her brother liked to move at a more leisurely pace than she did. "Aren't you worried about being late?"

"We've got an extra minute or two." He held the heavy door open for her. They entered a large, vaulted meeting room. "Come on, there's something I want to show you." He pulled her over to a massive stone fireplace and pointed upwards.

Her curiosity aroused, Carrie scanned the wall of knotted pine. Mounted on it was a display of antique guns.

"Are those loaded?" she asked him.

"No. A pin's been driven into the firing mechanism of each gun. The Golbins used to collect them. They're just for decoration." He nudged her elbow. "Look again. Do you see it?"

Carrie gasped. On the other side of the fireplace hung a tarnished horn.

Chapter 9

"A BUGLE!" Carrie exclaimed. "Oh my, a bugle!"

Now it was Sean's turn to smile. "I knew you'd be interested," he said. "I talked to the camp director. She says you can play 'Taps' tonight when it's time for light's out." He looked at her closely. "I know you're good, Carrie, but can you really play that old thing? It's not exactly the same as your trumpet."

"Of course I can play it. The main difference between a trumpet and a bugle is that a bugle doesn't have valves like a trumpet. You change the pitch by tightening your lips." She heaved a sigh of pure happiness. "Maybe Mrs. Delgado will let me play more than 'Taps.'"

"You can talk to her about it after dinner. See you later." Sean waved and was gone.

Carrie made her way through the throng to Tia's side. Megan reappeared. She moved close to Carrie, as if for protection.

A shrill whistle called everyone to order. Mrs. Delgado presented the staff. Carrie recognized some of them as teachers from her school. The camp director told the students how Mr. and Mrs. Golbin had bought the Haunted Ridge property for use as a campground.

Carrie let her mind wander. She was more interested in the camp's secrets than its history. She wondered about the reason behind the recent catastrophes. Did somebody want to shut the camp down? Who'd benefit from that? She had to find out!

The sound of scattered applause brought her thoughts back to the present. Mrs. Delgado introduced one of the men who had halted the buses in the meadow.

"This is Mr. Zeke Easley," she said, pointing to the man wearing the yellow bandanna. A smile lit up her pleasant face. "He's run a small, seasonal business here in the mountains for a long time. Five years ago he was joined by a partner, Mr. Harris. The two of them have been most generous with their time. They helped us prepare for your arrival. Zeke has also graciously agreed to lead us on a nature hike around the perimeter of the camp."

Zeke's companion stepped forward. "Call me Harry," he said with a merry twinkle in his eye. He stroked his short, curly beard. "It's an easy name to remember."

Laughter rippled through the crowd.

Mrs. Delgado spoke again. "Before we leave," she said, "there are three important rules I want to make certain you remember. Your teachers have gone over them with you many times in the past week. What are they?"

The students chanted in unison. "Stay on the path. Stay in the camp. Respect and protect the environment."

"Good," responded Mrs. Delgado. She beckoned to Sean. He held up a large picture showing green and red leaves in clusters of three. "What is this?" she asked them.

"Poison oak," they yelled back.

"Correct. It has been cleared off every trail within the boundaries of our camp. Obey the rules and it will not trouble you. Is there anything you'd like to add, Zeke?"

"Nope," he replied in a booming voice. "Just follow me." Zeke pulled his cowboy hat down lower on his forehead, then he raised his right arm high in the air.

Carrie thought he looked a bit like one of the cattle herders on those old western movies her dad liked to watch.

When Zeke was sure he had everyone's attention, he led them outdoors to the low mountain ridge that loomed behind the lodge. They hiked along a trail that sloped gently at first, then grew gradually steeper.

Tia lined her group up behind Mr. Lee. As they walked, he named the plants they passed. California wild rose and bracken fern bordered the pathway. To the students' left towered a stand of ponderosa pines. On their right, they could see the red-brown bark and shiny evergreen leaves of a madrone tree. It leaned against a tall

Douglas fir. Under the trees Carrie saw the arrow-shaped leaves of the trail marker plant. Mr. Lee explained that it was too late in the year for wild flowers. They bloomed in the spring and early summer.

Carrie glimpsed fluttering strips of scarlet material near the top of the ridge. Tia told her those were flags to mark the property line.

Jillian fingered her silver locket, rubbing it nervously. "I'll bet this place is crawling with bugs," she muttered.

"There are many insects in the forest," agreed Mr. Lee. "If you look closely, you might see centipedes, wood grubs, dragonflies, and banana slugs in their natural habitat."

Jillian moaned. "I hate bugs, I hate bugs, I HATE bugs," she muttered.

"Stop saying that!" Raven hissed.

"Why do you worry so much about insects?" asked Carrie in a puzzled voice. "Most of them are harmless."

"Is that so? I got stung once by a bee on my forehead," retorted Jillian. "My whole face swelled up like a balloon and turned bright purple."

"That is so gross!" Raven said in disgust. "Can't we talk about something else?"

Tia looked at Jillian with concern. "You must be allergic to insect stings. Did you tell the camp nurse?"

"I think my mom wrote it on my field trip permission slip. Why? Is it important?"

"Yes!" Tia exclaimed. "Next time you get stung, you might have a worse reaction!"

Everyone except Mr. Lee fell silent after that.

Carrie drew a deep breath, filling her lungs with clean, fresh air. It smelled especially sweet to her after the heavy scent of Jillian's perfume.

The trail forked periodically, but Zeke always seemed to know which way to go. Carrie was glad they had a guide. She thought it would be awfully easy to get lost without one.

A few minutes later, they changed direction again. Instead of continuing north along the ridge, the path turned downward. Most of the students were out of breath from their climb. Even Mr. Lee puffed a little. Now they walked with care. They crossed a small gully on a bridge made of rope-bound logs, then climbed down steps chiseled out of bare dirt. In some places, the rust-colored earth was slick. Carrie had to grab hold of a root to keep from falling, when all of a sudden, Beth lost her balance and slid into her.

"Watch out," grumbled Raven. "You almost bumped me."

"Oh!" Beth gasped. "I'm sorry."

"Don't worry about it."

After helping Beth to her feet, Carrie lifted her head and listened. She heard more than just the usual woodland noises. "What's that?" she asked.

"It's the sound of rushing water," Tia told her. "We're getting near the creek."

Carrie's heart beat faster. That meant they weren't far from the dam. Here, at last, was a chance to do some real sleuthing! Whoever had flooded the meadow must have left some trace behind. If she searched the area, she might find a clue to the vandal's identity! Her steps quickened with excitement.

After rounding a bend in the trail, the students found themselves on the gravelly shore of the creek. A mid-sized pond had been formed by damming the stream with timbers.

"Mr. Lee, can we stop for a short while?" asked Carrie. "It will give us time to catch our breath. I'm sure there's plenty of interesting things to see here," she added hopefully.

Mr. Lee agreed that it wouldn't hurt to linger. "We were near the head of the line. It won't matter if a few groups pass us," he said as he took a seat on an old pine stump. The others sat down on a log.

Megan wrapped her arms around her thin body. She hadn't said a word since before the hike began. Now she shivered, even though the day was still warm.

Carrie prowled the narrow beach. She knew she wouldn't have very long to search. She pawed through cattails and clumps of willows without discovering anything more exciting than a wrinkled piece of brightly colored foil. It didn't seem like much, but she put it into the pocket of her pants. "It might be evidence," she told herself stubbornly. "I won't give up." She was careful to avoid the patches of poison oak that also grew near the water.

She'd expected to find footprints. However, none showed in the rocky stream bed or on the chunks of milky-white quartz that lined its sides. She checked the wet sand near the edge of the dam itself, but too many feet had trampled it during the morning's repairs. No individual prints were visible. Refusing to be discouraged, Carrie hunted up and down the shoreline, seeking clues. She didn't know exactly what she was looking for, just anything that seemed out of place.

By now the other girls had taken note of her activities.

"What are you doing?" asked Jillian. She popped another stick of gum in her mouth.

"Just looking around," said Carrie. She blushed when she noticed the mocking smile on Raven's face.

"Yes," said Beth, "but looking for what?"

Carrie was saved from having to answer by Tia saying in a horrified voice, "Jillian! Remember the rule? Respect and protect the environment. Don't litter!" Tia shook her head so hard, her braids danced. She scooped up the gum wrapper Jillian had discarded and handed it back to her.

"We must go now," announced Mr. Lee, "or we will be left behind." He beckoned to the girls.

Carrie sighed. She was sure she'd missed something important. She started to follow the others. Suddenly, out of the corner of her eye, she caught the glitter of something gold in the shallows at the pond's rim. She wheeled around and dashed back across the beach.

Chapter 10

CARRIE KNELT DOWN at the edge of the pool. Being careful not to get her cast wet, she thrust her right arm in up to the elbow. Mud and silt clouded her view. Finally her fingers felt something metallic. She pulled the object out of the water.

"Got it!" she exclaimed aloud. She shook the water off, then dropped it in disappointment. "Darn! It's only a dented can." She shrugged her shoulders. "Well, I can't leave it here. It's trash." She crushed the can flat and tucked it in her pocket. She decided to throw it away when she returned to camp.

She leaped to her feet and ran to rejoin her group. To her dismay, they were out of sight. She couldn't see them anywhere. How she wished she'd asked them to wait for her! She called Tia's name, but there was no answer. They'd walked out of earshot, as well.

Carrie stood rigidly still, her hands clenched at her sides. She wasn't sure what to do. The trail branched off in three directions. One path followed the shoreline. Another rose up the hillside, and the third curved to the right.

"Oh, Lord," she whispered, "which way should I take?" She closed her eyes and concentrated. They'd just hiked down the ridge, so it couldn't be the one in the middle. Perhaps they were supposed to go upstream. Almost of their own accord, her feet turned to the right.

The route she'd chosen led her away from both the mountain and the creek. Hoping to catch up with the others, she set off at a brisk pace. The track grew narrower and narrower. Soon it was nothing more than a faint footpath. It ended in a field of ruins.

Carrie was more confused than ever. She'd been certain that this was the way she should go, but it seemed to lead nowhere. She shaded her eyes with her hand and looked out over the area.

Broken chimneys rose out of the grass. Eroded foundations and crumbling walls marked long-gone home sites. In some spots she saw dark, gaping holes that had once been basements. The only sound was the rustle of small, unseen animals scurrying through the rubble.

Carrie crept forward. What was this? Mrs. Delgado hadn't mentioned anything about it when she detailed the camp's history.

She walked between piles of tumbled boards. She was careful not to step on the rotting wood. It looked treacherous. She noticed a sheet of paper that the wind had pinned against a rusty nail. "More trash," she thought, and stuffed it into her pocket. A few ramshackle houses still stood upright. Carrie peeked into the dark, empty rooms of one of them. There was nothing in it but spiders. She steered clear of the other buildings. They leaned at such a crazy angle that she was sure they had to be on the verge of collapse.

This must have been a mining town, she decided, or even a lumber camp. She wondered who had lived here, and why they had abandoned it. What a spooky place! At least now she had a good idea why the area around here was called Haunted Ridge.

A cool breeze lifted the hair off the back of her neck. She glanced upward. The afternoon sun was setting lower in the sky. "Oh, no!" she said to herself, "it's getting late. If I don't return soon, they'll send out a search party for me. How do I get out of here?" With a sinking heart, she realized she could no longer see the trail that had brought her from the dam. She didn't know how to find her way back.

She looked about. Forest lined the meadow on two sides. She didn't dare venture in there. She knew if she did that, she'd REALLY be lost. On the third side, near the foot of the mountain, she saw the shabby cabin she'd noticed when they came in on the bus. Not far from it stood a large, barn-like structure. It was hidden from the road by the mountain's curve. Despite its size, she wouldn't have noticed it at all if she hadn't been looking closely. The building was shaded by a tall canopy of trees and painted to blend in with the forest growth. She started towards it, then stopped. From that direction came the frenzied barking of dogs. Carrie liked most dogs, but these didn't sound at all friendly. She immediately hurried the other way, down the deeply-rutted road that split the ghost town in two.

The old road led out of the town. Carrie followed it until her path was blocked by a fallen pine. She clambered over it. Ahead of her loomed a double row of ancient apple trees. Beyond the trees she saw a cozy, white-trimmed house. Kevin's words echoed in her mind: "Have you ever met a real, live witch?" Her steps slowed.

She stopped beside a black oak at the edge of the track. A curious rectangle made of polished rocks lay at its base. A sudden chill snaked up her spine. Without being told, Carrie knew exactly what those stones marked—a grave. A slab of wood rested against the tree. It might once have had a name and a date carved on it, but now it was weathered smooth.

"What're you doing on my land, girl?" boomed a deep voice.

Carrie jumped in the air and spun around. She was so startled that her breath seemed to catch in her throat. She couldn't answer.

A gray-haired woman in a shapeless, blue gingham dress faced Carrie. She grasped a copper-tipped walking stick, holding it in front of her like a weapon.

"From that campground, aren't you?"

Carrie nodded.

"I knew it!" the woman responded in a tone of grim triumph. "I knew I'd have trouble when Hank Golbin reopened that camp-ground. Told him so, too. Didn't listen. Never does." Her jaw jutted forward. "I'm Miss Maggie Higginbotham," she said. "I live here alone. Don't bother no one. No one bothers me. I like it that way." She poked her staff at Carrie. "Why'd you ignore my sign?"

"What sign?"

"This one!" Miss Higginbotham marched over to a hand-printed sign that sat square in the middle of the road. Carrie had been so interested in the grave site that she'd paid no attention to it.

The woman tapped the lettering with her staff. "What does it say?" she demanded. "Tell me."

Carrie felt a familiar feeling of panic twisting through her. "I can't read this!" she thought in distress. "The words are too long. I'll never be able to sound them out!" To make matters worse, the shrubbery next to her quivered and she heard a faint, barely smothered giggle.

"Tell me!" Miss Higginbotham roared.

"On t-t-t," Carrie stuttered, then stopped.

"What? Something wrong with you? Can't you read it, girl? Can't you read it?"

Despite her embarrassment, Carrie looked the old woman straight in the eye. "No," she said evenly. "I can't."

Miss Higginbotham reared back. "Well!" she exclaimed. "What sass!" She struck the sign. "No trespassing. Violators will be prosecuted," she read out loud. Her stick stabbed each word for emphasis. "Knew I'd have problems when you kids came to camp. Didn't nobody tell you not to cross my property line?"

Carrie swallowed hard. "I don't see any markers. Where is your property line?"

"What? Course there's markers! Pounded them in myself!" Miss Higginbotham stomped along the road, poking her head in the bushes, tramping around the trees. "Where'd those dang things go?" she muttered. "Where'd they go?"

Carrie followed. Near a dogwood bush she noticed a suspicious looking bump sticking out of the ground. Carrie bent down and brushed the dirt away. She uncovered the sawed-off end of a post.

Before she could say anything, Kevin and Evan popped out from behind the trunk of a cedar tree.

Chapter 11

FOR THE SECOND TIME in ten minutes, Carrie jumped back in surprise. "What are you doing here?" she gasped.

"Watching you stand up to that witch," answered Kevin. He hunched his shoulders and thrust his chin out in imitation of Miss Higginbotham. "Can't you read it, girl, can't you read it?" he chanted.

"No, I can't," Evan mimicked Carrie. They both burst out laughing.

Carrie smiled weakly. "Believe me, boys, it wasn't that funny."

The old woman returned. "I see more trespassers," she growled.

Carrie quickly distracted her by pointing out the cut post end. Miss Higginbotham got down on her hands and knees to examine it. She mumbled hoarsely to herself.

The twins took advantage of the distraction and started running back to camp.

Carrie dashed after them. "Don't leave without me," she yelled.

"Why?" Kevin called over his shoulder. "Afraid you're going to get lost again?"

Evan waited for Carrie. "It's a good thing we showed up," he bragged, "or that witch might have had you for dinner!"

"Listen, you guys," said Carrie, "stop calling her that. Her name's Maggie Higginbotham. She's not a real witch. She just doesn't like visitors." Carrie rubbed the sweat off her forehead with the back of her arm. "How'd you two know where to find me?" she asked.

Kevin snickered. "We've been following you the whole time," he said.

"Yeah, we were so quiet, you didn't even hear us," added Evan. "It was great!"

Carrie was torn between gratitude and indignation. "Get me back to camp," she said, "and I'll forgive you."

Kevin's pace slowed when they came to the empty city in the field. "This is really creepy looking," he said with enthusiasm. "Let's explore."

Evan darted over to a ruined house.

"Hold it!" Carrie shouted. "That's not safe." She seized Evan by the shirttail. "You'll get hurt if the roof caves in," she said as she pulled him back.

"Aw, you worry too much," said Kevin. He teetered on a beam that stretched across a jumble of broken boards beside the house. "Look at me," he said. "I'm a tightrope walker. Bet you can't do this."

Carrie lunged after him. She heard the decaying lumber under Kevin's feet snap as she reached for him. She grabbed his arm and yanked hard. The two of them tumbled backwards, landing in a patch of prickly weeds. The pile of planks that had supported Kevin collapsed and crashed into a deep basement hole.

Evan peered downward. His face was white when he turned and looked back at his brother.

"Wow," he said in a awed voice. "You'd be smashed if you'd fallen in there with all that wood."

Carrie picked herself up and brushed off her pants. She was hot and tired, scratched and dirty.

"Let's get out of here," she said.

The boys showed her the trail back. They acted as anxious as she did to get away from the abandoned town and its hidden dangers.

"Kevin," Carrie said as they hurried down the grassy track, "what else did your parents tell you about the campground?"

Kevin's brow furrowed. "They said that things kept falling apart, or getting lost. The water turned funny colors."

"Yeah," agreed Evan, "like the camp was jinxed."

"Aren't they worried about letting you come here?" Carrie asked.

"They're not worried," Kevin assured her. "Why should they be? It was just small stuff that went wrong during the summer clean-up, nothing major."

"What did they say about the ghost town?"

Evan shook his head. "Nothing."

"Then why did they tell you about Miss Higginbotham?"

"Well, they didn't exactly tell us," admitted Kevin. "We overheard them talking to each other."

Carrie rolled her eyes. "So, you not only spy on me, you spy on your parents, as well. Did you hear them mention anyone else?"

"Remember those men who guided us on the hike?" asked Kevin.

"Zeke and Harry?"

"That's right. They came around a lot. They tried to fix the things that broke, but they weren't very good at it."

"It made our Pop mad," Evan said with relish. "They got in his way. He can fix ANYTHING."

"Where do they live?"

Evan gestured toward the base of the mountain.

"In that junky old shack," replied Kevin. "We passed their Christmas tree farm on the way into camp. They have dogs. Really BIG dogs. Hey! There's the creek. Hurry up!" He broke into a run.

"The dam is straight ahead," called out Evan.

Tia and Derek met them at the pond.

"Thank goodness!" Tia exclaimed. She rushed over and threw her arms around Carrie. "We didn't know where you were, or which way you'd gone. Sean and Mr. Lee have been out searching for you along the ridge trail."

Derek looked ready to explode.

"I'm sorry," Carrie said in a muffled voice. She twisted her hands together behind her back. "I got mixed up and took the wrong path."

Derek glowered at Kevin and Evan. "What's their excuse?" he snapped.

The two boys ducked behind Carrie. All her own irritation with the twins evaporated. After all, they had helped her.

"They rescued me," she told Derek. "Otherwise I'd still be out wandering around somewhere with no idea of how to get back to camp."

Derek's straight, black brows were drawn together in exasperation. "Do you expect me to believe that?" he demanded.

Carrie blushed. "I guess you don't know how easily I get lost. If it wasn't for my friend, Amy, I'd never be able to find my school locker," she said. "Or get it open, either," she added silently.

Derek's features relaxed slightly. "Sean told us your sense of direction is a little haywire."

Carrie's face felt even warmer. It was one thing to admit that on her own. It was quite another to discover that her brother had blabbed it to his friends.

"Tia," said Derek, "how about taking Kevin and Evan to see Mrs. Delgado? I need to talk to Carrie."

Evan took a quick step backward.

"But we don't WANT to see Mrs. Delgado," protested Kevin.

"Too bad," answered Derek without any sympathy in his voice, "she wants to see you."

Tia glanced at Derek's grim face. "You can come with me if you'd like, Carrie. Sean should be back by now. You don't have to stay and listen to Derek."

Carrie patted Tia on the shoulder. "Go ahead," she whispered. "He doesn't scare me."

Derek waited until Tia and the twins walked out of sight, then he lashed out at Carrie. "Don't you have any sense at all?" he asked furiously. "Tia and I got into a lot of trouble because of you."

"I said I was sorry! I didn't do it on purpose." It had never occurred to her that the counselors might suffer because of her mistake. Carrie felt hot tears prickling behind her eyelids. She blinked them angrily away.

"When you get lost, you're supposed to stay put!" he said. "Don't move until you're found."

"I know. That's what the leaders at girls camp taught us." She bit her lip. How could she explain to Derek that her steps had been guided to the ghost town? She knew the Lord meant her to go there. She just didn't know the reason why yet.

Derek folded his arms across his chest. He scowled at her. "Why don't you admit it? You were hunting for clues," he said in an accusing voice.

Carrie's eyes widened.

"I thought so! Next time tell someone where you're going before you disappear," he shouted.

"Stop yelling!" Carrie lifted her chin. "I didn't know where I was going until I got there," she said with as much dignity as she could muster. She brushed past Derek and started walking.

"You're going the wrong way again!" he said bitterly. "Camp's in the other direction."

She gritted her teeth. Why in the world did he have to be so aggravating?

"You'd better come with me. Mrs. Delgado wants to talk to you, too." Derek stalked off.

Carrie followed. Her shorter, quicker steps kept up with his long strides. A nervous feeling settled in the pit of her stomach. She wasn't looking forward at all to the coming interview. Her heart seemed to beat louder the closer they got to camp. If she couldn't explain to Derek why she'd wandered off, what was she going to tell Mrs. Delgado?

Chapter 12

SEAN MET THEM at the entrance to the lodge. The relief on his face eased some of the sting of Derek's sharp words. Her brother was so obviously happy to see her that Carrie's spirits rose slightly.

The twins slunk past as he opened the door.

"Good luck," called out Kevin.

Evan waved. Carrie noticed that the glint of mischief was back in his eyes. He and his brother scurried over to their cabin. Derek sped after them.

"What's going to happen now?" Carrie asked Sean. "Is Mrs. Delgado mad at me? Derek sure was!"

"He was worried, Carrie. We all were."

"Oh."

Sean flashed Carrie another reassuring grin. "Everything will be all right," he said. "I promise. Go on up to Mrs. Delgado's office. It's on the second floor."

Carrie entered the building. At the rear of the meeting hall, a spiral staircase wound upwards to a second-story balcony. Beyond the balcony, a light shone through an open doorway. "I'd better get this over with," she thought. "Waiting won't help." She climbed the stairs to a large, wood-paneled room. On its far wall she saw a beautifully-detailed map.

Mrs. Delgado greeted her warmly. She offered Carrie a mint, then introduced her to a slender man with sun-bleached hair.

"This is Mr. J. R. Golbin, she said. "His family owns the campground."

"Ah," he said lightly, "our wanderer returns."

Carrie shook the hand he held out to her. Even though he wore a courteous expression on his tanned face, he managed to give an impression of barely concealed disdain.

Mrs. Delgado sat down behind an enormous desk. Mr. Golbin pushed the telephone to one side, then perched casually on the desk's flat top.

Carrie settled into a leather chair. She still felt nervous but, to her relief, Mrs. Delgado didn't delve too closely into her reasons for getting lost.

"It is especially important," Mrs. Delgado concluded after a gentle scolding, "that each student stay within the camp boundaries. There are ruins nearby which could be quite hazardous."

Mr. Golbin leaned back and crossed his arms. "We should have knocked those old buildings down a long time ago. However, my folks felt they were of historical interest. They fenced them off instead."

Carrie stopped squirming. "Really? The fence is gone, too," she told him.

Mr. Golbin looked amused, as if she had just said something silly.

"You spoke as if the fence isn't the only thing that's missing. What else has disappeared?" Mrs. Delgado asked in a troubled voice.

"The boundary markers!" Carrie blurted out. She gazed up into Mr. Golbin's skeptical face. "Somebody chopped down the posts between the campground and the ghost town, as well as between the town and Miss Higginbotham's property. The same person must have taken down the fence. It's vanished! There's no trace of it anywhere."

Mrs. Delgado gripped the edge of the desk so tight that the knuckles on her hands showed white. "You actually got close to the ruins? Carrie, stay away from there!"

"I know they're dangerous," Carrie admitted.

"You don't know how dangerous!" Mr. Golbin slid off the desk top. "I'll investigate this. If it is true, the fence will be rebuilt and the boundary markers reset. If it isn't true," he said, looking intently at Carrie, "you're in deep trouble, young lady!" He headed for the door.

"Please, wait," Carrie begged. "Would you tell me something before you go?" Even though he made her feel uncomfortable, she didn't want to lose the chance to ask a few questions.

"Make it quick."

"Why did your family close the campground?"

"Lots of little things happened the last year we operated it. Nothing real serious, just one annoying problem after another," he said. "Then one summer evening my father went riding through the ghost town." The tone of his voice was no longer light. It was clipped and bitter. "Something spooked Dad's horse. The frightened animal crashed into one of those rotting shanties. The whole building fell. The horse broke its leg and had to be shot. My dad's injuries were so severe that he required constant care for the next several months. After coping with that, my mother felt unable to face the challenge of running the camp alone."

Carrie gasped. Kevin's near-accident was still fresh in her mind. She could guess why the fence and boundary markers had been torn down. If one of the students wandered into the ruined city and got hurt, the campground would be forced to shut down again immediately.

"Why didn't you take over the camp, Mr. Golbin?" she asked after a short pause.

At first Carrie thought he wasn't going to answer. At last he said, "My parents put a lot of time and energy into running this place. I'm not interested in doing that."

He slammed the door as he went out.

Mrs. Delgado stared after him. She remained seated, her hands still gripping the desk.

"We must make this experiment work," she said earnestly. "If too many things go wrong this week, the Golbins will be reluctant to let us hold another outdoor classroom here again. Their son already wants to sell the campground. He's trying to talk them out of donating it for school use."

Carrie couldn't resist trying to get more information. "Mrs. Delgado," she began hesitantly, "I saw an old grave site on Miss Higginbotham's land."

"So, you met our neighbor, Maggie Higginbotham." Mrs. Delgado's lips twisted into a thin smile. "She tends to discourage visitors."

Carrie grinned back. "I can tell you've met her, too." She rested her chin on the palm of her hand. "Do you know who's buried in that grave?" she asked.

"No," Mrs. Delgado replied, "I don't. In fact, I don't believe anyone living does know. It's probably a prospector, or somebody who once lived in that abandoned town. Miss Higginbotham tends the grave."

"How long has she lived around here?"

"For most of her life. She was here long before the Golbins came to Haunted Ridge."

"Do you know anyone else who'd like to see the camp closed?"

Mrs. Delgado appeared surprised. "No, of course not."

"What about Harry and Zeke? When did you meet them?"

"In August." Mrs. Delgado sighed. "They've been so helpful. They did tell me, though, that the camp has always had problems. I wish I'd known that before I agreed to take this job. I might have been better prepared. You wouldn't believe some of the things that have happened. I lost the cabin assignment list, the menu plan disappeared, and I've had to screw my desk back together three times already."

"I had a hard time convincing my little sister we wouldn't be enjoying the company of ugly little elves. She calls this the goblin's campground."

A smile returned to the camp director's face. "How apt," she said. "Sometimes it seems as if that's what I'm dealing with here." Mrs. Delgado tucked a stray lock of hair back into her bun. She stood up. "Well, Carrie, it's almost dinner time. You'd better go. By the way," she added with a twinkle in her eye, "your brother tells me you might be willing to play 'Taps' for us at ten o'clock tonight."

"Oh, yes! Do I get to play some other songs as well?"

"Certainly. I'm glad to see such enthusiasm. You can pick up the bugle after the campfire gathering."

Carrie left the office with a cheerful heart. As she skipped down the stairs, her cast bumped against the bulge in her pocket. She remembered the trash she had found. There had to be a wastebasket around here someplace. She walked back through the meeting hall. On the way, she met Beth Astin, her arms full of books.

"What are you looking for now?" Beth asked.

"A wastebasket." Carrie pulled the squashed can from her pocket and held it out to show Beth. "I picked this up on the hike. Do you know where I can toss it?"

"There's a trash bin by the front door."

"Thanks." Carrie grinned from ear to ear. "You don't have to tell me what you've been doing," she said.

Beth beamed back at her. "Did you see the bookshelves beside the fireplace?" she asked happily.

Carrie shook her head. She'd had eyes only for the bugle.

"There are four whole shelves filled with paperbacks, and I don't think I've read a single one of them before!" Beth exclaimed. "They all look interesting. I'm going to see how many I can read before we go home."

"It'd take me a lifetime to plow through that many books," Carrie said ruefully. She threw the can away as they left the lodge. She kept the paper and scrap of foil, though. Perhaps she'd have a chance to examine them later. The piece of paper had writing on it. If it was too difficult to decipher, she'd give it to Sean to figure out.

The two girls walked outside together. A cool wind rustled through the pines and stirred the dry leaves along the pathway. Carrie decided to put her sweatshirt back on when they got back to the cabin.

She wrinkled her nose and made a face when they reached their cabin. "I'm almost afraid to look inside," she said. She poked her head through the doorway, then heaved a huge sigh of relief. "Everything looks fine. Thank goodness!"

"You can say that again!" Beth set the books up on top of her cupboard. "You didn't really make that terrible mess earlier, did you, Carrie?"

"No!"

"I shouldn't have jumped to conclusions this morning. I'm sorry."

"That's okay. I understand. It did look kind of suspicious." Carrie felt as if a big burden had just been lifted off her shoulders. Now if only the other girls would believe her!

Beth twisted a long strand of golden brown hair between her fingers. She stared at the floor, as if embarrassed to tell Carrie what she had to say next.

"There's a lot of rumors flying around camp. Somebody's been telling everyone that you trashed our cabin."

Carrie's heart seemed to plummet all the way down to her shoes. When she had learned there was a mystery to be solved, she hadn't expected to be one of the suspects!

Chapter 13

CARRIE SHOOK BETH GENTLY by the arm. "You must have some idea what's going on around here. You know the other students better than I do."

Beth glanced up. "Not exactly," she admitted. A faint flush spread across her face.

"But..."

Raven's harsh voice cut into the conversation. "Haven't you heard? Beth's so smart," she said as she entered the cabin, "that her only friends are little sixth-graders." She walked over to the tiny mirror and wound another ribbon around her sleek, black ponytail. She looked over her shoulder at Carrie. "Remember, introduce me to Derek. Do it tonight." She left the cabin without waiting for a response.

Carrie cleared her throat. "Don't let Raven bother you," she said quietly. "She gets a kick out of needling people." Picking up a container of mosquito repellent, she rubbed the lotion all over her arms, ankles, face and neck. She held the bottle out to Beth. "Want some? We'll probably need it before the day's over."

"No, thanks. I've already sprayed on enough to kill a whole army of mosquitos." Beth thumbed the pages of one of the novels she had selected to read, then put the book aside. "I guess I ought to explain to you what Raven was talking about," she said. "Last year I was in the fifth grade. I skipped."

"Wow!" Carrie was impressed. "You MUST be smart. You shouldn't have any trouble at all making new friends."

Beth's flush deepened. "Look," she said, peering at Carrie over the tops of her glasses, "this may sound conceited, but I know I'm smart. I like being able to learn quickly and memorize easily. I just can't stand being labeled 'Beth, the brain,' or 'Beth, the bookworm.'" She pushed her glasses back up to the bridge of her nose. "I don't mind helping people with their homework, but I hate it when they make fun of me afterward."

Carrie nodded in sympathy. "My brother skipped a grade, too. He can't stand being called 'Einstein.' It's one of the few things that bother him." She giggled. "Do you realize we share a similar predicament? Your friends are still in the sixth grade and, except for Amy, all my school friends are eighth-grade band members. So, here we both are, stuck in the woods with a bunch of seventh-graders. Aren't we lucky!" She grabbed her sweatshirt. "Come on," she said. "I think I heard the dinner bell. Let's find Megan. It's time to eat."

They met Megan in the kitchen area. She didn't answer when Carrie asked where she had been. Instead she silently helped Carrie slip on her sweatshirt.

"Thanks," Carrie said gratefully. "I'll be glad when I can finally get this cast off. It really gets in the way sometimes."

Megan smiled. "It's a good thing you're right-handed," she said.

Jillian cut into line behind Beth. She watched Megan carry her dinner to the table, then spoke to Carrie. "Raven says Megan's a loser."

It was obvious that Megan heard. Her shoulders hunched, as if she was expecting a blow.

"Raven says a lot of things," replied Carrie, "most of them mean!"

Jillian blew a big bubble and let it pop. "Aren't you scared that if you hang around with Megan, people will think you're a loser, too?" she asked.

Carrie thought about how she had walked past Megan on the bus because she was afraid of being teased. The memory shamed her. She shook her head.

"No," she answered. She piled her plate high with hot dogs and chili beans. "That's not the kind of thing I want to waste my time worrying about. Besides, I don't think Megan's a loser. Raven ought to keep her mouth shut!" Carrie scooped up utensils and a cup, then went to sit down beside Megan. They were soon joined by the rest of their cabin mates.

As they ate, Raven entertained them with a funny, scary story. The tale was not only wickedly hilarious, but it sent chills up and down Carrie's spine. She was certain she'd remember it late into the night. She also noticed that all during the meal Raven never seemed to take her eyes off Megan. An image flashed through Carrie's mind of a large, dark bird preparing to swoop down on its prey.

Megan and Raven both disappeared while the others took care of their dishes.

"Don't forget," said Tia, "it's our cabin's turn for kitchen duty tomorrow before breakfast.

Jillian pouted. "I'd planned to sleep in."

"Don't count on it," Tia said firmly. "I'll wake you up." She left to go visit with two of the other counselors.

Carrie hadn't met either one of them before. She asked Jillian their names.

"That's Bee and Chou Vang," answered Jillian. "Tia's family sponsored their family's trip to the United States. They've been good friends for a long time."

"Oh." Carrie pocketed an extra handful of cookies. She wished she could talk to Amy. Jillian seemed to know almost everything about everybody, just like Amy did. Jillian was pleasant enough most of the time, too. However, she didn't have Amy's kind heart and strong spirit. Carrie sighed. "Does anyone know where Megan went?" she asked. "I need to talk to her."

Jillian looked bored. She popped another stick of gum in her mouth and walked away.

"We know, we know," chanted Kevin. He appeared suddenly by Carrie's side. "If we tell you, will you give us more candy?"

"How about some Oreos instead?" She held out a couple of cream-filled chocolate cookies.

"It's a deal," said Kevin.

Evan snatched the cookies from Carrie's hand. He passed one to his brother, then pointed across the clearing.

"We saw her run off towards the meadow," said Kevin.

"Yeah. Someone was following her," added Evan.

Carrie felt a sense of urgency without knowing exactly why. "Listen, I need the two of you to do me a favor. Tell Tia I went down to the meadow after Megan. Make sure she knows where I am so she doesn't worry."

Evan giggled. "Are you going to get lost again?"

"Of course not!" Carrie turned to leave.

"Wait! You're headed the wrong way," protested Kevin. "You need to take that dirt road over there, the one that goes by the boys' cabins."

Evan spun her around and gave her a push in the right direction. "We could go with you," he offered hopefully.

"No, thanks. I can manage by myself." Carrie crossed the clearing at a run and sped past the cabins.

Fortunately the road was easy to find. It only took her a few minutes to arrive at the creek. She stopped to catch her breath on the bridge. She leaned against its rough, wooden railing and looked around.

She saw Megan on the opposite bank of the creek, backed up against a bay tree. Raven was talking to her in a low, vicious voice. As Carrie sprinted toward them, Raven gave Megan a sharp, stinging slap across the face.

"Hey! Stop that!" Carrie shouted.

Raven drew back her arm again. Carrie grabbed Megan and jerked her out of the way. Raven hit the tree instead.

"Ow!" wailed Raven. She hopped around, cradling her sore hand. She stumbled into a thorny blackberry bush and howled again in pain. "Mind your own business!" she raged. "Stay out of this!"

Carrie refused to be intimidated. "Not a chance," she said. "You leave Megan alone!"

"I'll push you in the creek!" Raven said furiously. "Your cast will get wet. You'll get in trouble and have to go home."

Carrie moved backwards, towards the water. She kept her eyes on Raven's face.

Raven lowered her head and charged. At the last moment, Carrie stepped aside. Raven's forward momentum carried her over the bank. She fell headfirst into the creek.

Raven struggled to her feet, gasping and coughing. Water

streamed from her clothes. Mud dripped from her hair. She reached for Carrie, her fingers curled like claws.

Chapter 14

CARRIE DECIDED THAT A HASTY RETREAT was the wisest strategy. She whirled around and ran right smack into Derek.

Derek steadied her, then jerked his head toward the soggy figure rising out of the creek. "Who's that?" he asked curtly.

Carrie remembered the promise she had made. "Meet Raven Blake," she said.

Raven pointed a wet, trembling finger at Carrie and ordered, "Report her to the camp director at once! She pushed me into the brook."

Carrie was taken aback by the anger blazing in Derek's eyes, until she realized it wasn't directed at her.

"I saw what happened. You got exactly what you deserved!" he said roughly. He grabbed Carrie's arm. "Let's get out of here. I can't say much for the company you keep."

"Wait. Where's Megan?"

Derek shrugged. "She's gone."

Raven hauled herself out of the water. Her shoes made squishing noises as she stomped away.

"You're going to have problems with her," Derek warned.

Carrie didn't even want to think about that. "What were you doing out here in the meadow?" she asked instead.

"I overheard you talking to the twins. I thought you might need help, so I followed you," Derek replied. To Carrie's surprise, he smiled at her. "Sean keeps telling me you can take care of yourself. I don't know why I have such a hard time believing him."

The two of them crossed the bridge together. Carrie saw a red-tailed hawk circling overhead. She wondered if it was returning to its nest. As the sun set lower in the sky, the shadows lengthened. Swarms of mosquitos hovered in the air.

"It's a good thing I put on mosquito repellent," she said.

Derek swatted at a bug. "I wish I had! I'm going back to the cabin to get some. I need to check on those boys anyway. They're probably up to no good." He stopped in the middle of the tree-shaded road. "How about letting me know how to tell the twins apart? I don't like putting up with a lot of nonsense. It'd help a lot if I could call them by name."

"All you have to do is watch them. Kevin speaks first. Evan always acts first."

"Is that so? Great! Say, can you find your way to that boulder behind the lodge? I told Tia you'd be there."

"Of course," she answered indignantly. "How hard can it be? The lodge is in plain sight, and I am not..."

"Helpless," he finished for her. "Okay. Stay out of trouble."

"That sounds like good advice," she said with a laugh.

Derek ran on ahead.

As soon as he disappeared around the bend, Megan materialized out from behind a maple tree. Her face was tear-stained and blotchy.

Carrie was so relieved to see her that she invited Megan to come with her to meet Sean.

Megan hung back. "He won't want to see me."

"Sure he will," Carrie said with the assurance born of past experience. "My brother likes just about anybody." She shifted her weight from one foot to the other while Megan hesitated. "Would you rather wait here for Raven to find you?" she demanded impatiently.

Megan ducked her head. "No," she muttered.

"All right. Let's go."

As the two girls hiked back to the main part of camp, they heard a movement in the leaves.

"Oh, look!" exclaimed Megan. She stopped to let a long, yellow-and black-striped snake slither across their path.

Carrie gulped. "Is it poisonous?" she whispered anxiously.

"No, I don't think so," Megan whispered back.

Carrie watched it glide into the wild strawberry plants along the side of the road. She glanced at Megan. There was no fear in the other girl's eyes, just interest in the snake's fluid beauty. Carrie was amazed.

"Seeing a big snake like that at close range would scare a lot of people," she commented.

"What did you expect me to do? Scream?" Megan's mouth curved upward in shy amusement. "It's only people that frighten me," she said quietly. Her smile widened. "Guess what? I saw a family of skunks just before dinner."

"Now don't tell me that didn't scare you!"

"I didn't bother them and they didn't bother me. The woods are full of interesting things."

Carrie wrinkled her forehead. "I don't understand," she said. "Why were you so nervous on the hike if things like snakes and skunks don't worry you?"

Megan picked up a stick and concentrated on the path without answering Carrie.

The two girls stopped at the washroom to clean up, then headed for the lodge.

"I know where that rock is that your friend mentioned. Want me to show you?" inquired Megan.

"Sure."

Sean was waiting for them. Carrie introduced him to Megan.

"Megan Zeller," he repeated thoughtfully, just as Carrie had on the bus. "That's an unusual last name." His face lit up. "I think I've met your grandfather. He owns a novelty shop on Center Street, doesn't he?"

Megan nodded.

"One of the illusions that he sells is called 'Megan's Crystal.' He told me he named it after his granddaughter. I haven't figured out yet how it works."

Megan beamed back at him, her bashfulness forgotten. "You'll have to buy it first. Grandpa will be glad to explain it to you then."

Sean laughed good-naturedly. "You're probably right," he said. He sat down cross-legged on the boulder. He and Megan happily discussed her grandfather's business.

Once more Carrie was astonished at the knack her brother had for putting people at ease. She wished she shared it. She hadn't had any success whatsoever in getting Megan to answer a direct question.

Derek appeared several minutes later, looking morose. "It doesn't work," he announced gloomily, sitting down beside Megan on a fallen log.

Carrie blinked. What on earth was he talking about?

"I haven't the patience to wait and see which twin does what first. They get into mischief too fast. Isn't there a simpler way to tell those two imps apart?"

"Are you talking about Kevin and Evan Thornberg? I can help you out," volunteered Sean.

Derek brightened immediately.

"Evan parts his hair on the right side because he's left-handed. Kevin parts his hair on the left. He's right-handed."

Derek reached into his shirt pocket for paper and pen. "This is REALLY going to make my job easier," he said gratefully. He wrote down what Sean had said.

Carrie kept her eyes on the ground. She had the awful feeling that Derek wondered why she hadn't been as observant as Sean. She hoped her brother wouldn't mention that she had a hard time telling right from left.

Derek finished writing. "Tell me something else," he said, staring Carrie straight in the eye. "Why are you so set on playing detective? You shouldn't try to show off." He let his gaze travel down to her cast. "You might get hurt."

"I am NOT trying to show off!" Carrie retorted. She hoped her face wasn't turning beet red. "I need to solve the mystery. Otherwise, the rest of the students will go on thinking I'm stupid. I'd like to make a few friends while we're here at camp."

Megan looked surprised.

Sean frowned. "We don't think you're stupid."

Carrie glanced at Derek.

He stretched his long legs out in front of him. "Don't look at me," he said. "I may have gotten irritated with you on occasion, but I never thought you were stupid, either."

Carrie raised her eyebrows. She didn't believe him.

"Well, not recently," he insisted. "Not since…"

"Not since you saw me solve Mrs. Markowski's mystery," Carrie finished for him. "See what I mean?"

"That's crazy," Derek said bluntly. "Are you saying that Amy only likes you because she thinks you're Sherlock Holmes?"

"No," admitted Carrie.

"You are good at figuring things out," said Sean. "I think it's a gift you have, like your musical talent, or the way you can remember practically anything you hear. However, it doesn't have anything to do with making friends."

Carrie's mouth set in a stubborn line. She wasn't about to give up, no matter what they said!

"There's another reason I need to find out what's going on around here," she confessed. "I'm getting blamed for part of the trouble." She told them about the mayhem in her cabin and the rumors that Beth said were spreading through the camp.

"We'll have to fix that," responded Sean. He ran both hands through his dark red hair. "Okay. Carrie wants to solve a mystery. Let's pool our information. We know that somebody has been causing trouble at the campground. My guess is that they're trying to shut it down."

"Why?" challenged Derek. "Why would anyone want to close the camp?"

Sean showed them a scrap of lumber. "I found this when we worked on the dam. I think it's part of an old signpost." He handed it to Derek. The other boy and Megan examined it together before passing it on.

Carrie put her finger under the two short words that had been burned into the wood and slowly sounded them out. "Gold Creek," she said triumphantly. "That must be the name of the stream."

Derek's dark blue eyes were puzzled. "That still doesn't tell us why..."

"Oh yes it does!" shouted Carrie. She clapped her hand over her mouth. She hadn't meant to yell. "I'll bet there's a big gold deposit on Haunted Ridge," she continued in a softer voice. "Someone wants us out of the way so they can search our campsite for it."

"That's exactly what I thought," said Sean.

Carrie suddenly remembered the paper she had found earlier. She pulled it out of her pocket and handed it to Sean. "I discovered this while I was lost," she announced.

"What is it?" asked Derek.

"You tell him, Sean," Carrie said quickly. "I haven't had time to look at it yet."

"It's a treasure map," Sean exclaimed, his voice sharp with excitement, "a real, honest-to-goodness treasure map!"

Chapter 15

SEAN TURNED THE MAP AROUND so they could all see it. "Look at all these X's," he said, "I'll bet they mark spots where gold is buried!"

Carrie looked. Black X's formed a rough semi-circle on the paper. Beside each X was a hand-drawn symbol. She pointed to one of them.

"What do these little drawings mean?" she asked.

"They must be landmarks," Sean said. "See, this looks like a tree stump. This one looks like a large rock…"

"That's right!" interrupted Derek. He bent forward. "There's a bridge, a gate, some kind of a building, and that looks like two trees leaning together."

The boys pored over the map, their heads close together, puzzling out the rest of the symbols. Carrie sat back on her heels and watched them. She was troubled. The things they described didn't fit with what she had learned in school about gold mining in the Sierra Nevada mountains. Maybe they had made a mistake. She was hesitant to speak up, however. Sean was a straight-A student. She wasn't anxious to appear foolish by disagreeing with him, especially in front of Megan and Derek.

"We ought to talk to Mrs. Delgado about this," she said.

"I'll take care of that," volunteered Sean. "Do you mind if I take the map to show her?"

"Go ahead." Carrie paused. The uneasy feeling she had wouldn't leave. "But we'd better be careful," she warned, "so we don't stumble into something dangerous."

"All we have to do is keep our eyes and ears open. What could be dangerous about that?" reasoned Sean. "After all, nothing too terrible has happened so far. It's just little stuff gone wrong."

Carrie thought of Mr. Golbin's evening ride through the ghost town. She wasn't so sure. What if Sean was being overconfident?

Derek brushed his hair out of his eyes. "Wrecking the dam wasn't such a little thing," he answered in a serious voice.

"Nobody was hurt," responded Sean, "and it only took a morning to fix."

"We're lucky they haven't done something REALLY awful, like burning down the whole camp!" Derek exclaimed.

"That won't happen. Anyone involved in illegal mining won't want to do anything serious enough to bring the sheriff around. They'd have to be crazy to risk a full-scale investigation." Sean paused. "If the campground is hit by a string of minor problems, the parents will blame the staff. The staff will blame Mrs. Delgado. Mrs. Delgado will blame the Golbins and..."

"Next year's seventh-graders won't get to come here," concluded Carrie. She told the other three about her meeting with Miss Higginbotham and her interview with J. R. Golbin.

The ghost of a smile crossed Megan's face as Carrie mimicked Miss Higginbotham's staccato speech.

"Do you think one of them is causing the trouble?" Derek asked.

"It's possible," answered Sean. "We have a motive. Now let's list suspects." He held up one finger. "First, there's J. R. Golbin. According to Mrs. Delgado, he wants to sell the campground. Maybe he has inside information about mineral deposits." He held up another finger. "Second, there's Miss Higginbotham. She didn't want the camp to reopen. I think that's pretty suspicious."

"Not all the teachers are happy with the way Mrs. Delgado is running things," Derek informed them. "A few claim they could do better. And what about those two men, Zeke and Harry? They might have found out about the gold."

Carrie dismissed the idea. "I doubt it's them. Mrs. Delgado says they've offered her plenty of assistance."

"That's true," agreed Sean. "They gave us a hand when we fixed the dam."

Derek snorted. "Some help they were! Most of the time they just got in the way."

Sean laughed. "So they weren't very good at it. At least they tried. That ought to count for something."

"What about one of the students?" Carrie asked. She thought of Raven.

The boys appeared skeptical, but they admitted it was a remote possibility. "Very remote," said Derek.

Carrie reached into her pocket again. She took out the wrinkled piece of foil she had found among the cattails at the edge of the pond.

Sean picked it up and sniffed it. "This smells like candy," he said.

"Let me see that," demanded Derek. He inspected it closely. "I know what this is. It's the inside wrapper from a roll of Mint Dreams."

"Do you remember seeing anyone eat that kind of candy?" Carrie asked. "We might be able to add another suspect to our list."

"Mrs. Delgado eats those all the time," Sean replied with a broad smile, "especially when she's nervous. She has a sweet tooth."

"Maybe she caused the dam disaster," Carrie blurted out.

"Don't be ridiculous!" snapped Derek. "I like that kind of candy, too, and I didn't knock down the dam." He jumped up.

Carrie glared at him.

"Calm down, you two," said Sean. "Carrie and Megan, see if you can narrow down our list of suspects. Keep your ears open for information about the Golbins and the history of Haunted Ridge. Derek, listen to the staff members. Find out if any of them are interested in minerals or mining. I'm going to investigate a couple of maps." He looked at his watch. "It's about time for campfire. Let's meet back here tomorrow night at the same time. We'll compare notes then."

Carrie pulled Megan to her feet. The other girl hadn't spoken a word since they had started discussing the mystery. She'd just sat with her head down and her hands clasped tightly together. The scarlet spot where Raven struck her stood out like a badge on her pale face.

"Let's go," Carrie urged. They walked single file along the path to the clearing. Carrie slowed down enough to let the boys move on ahead, out of earshot. "Megan," she whispered, "we should tell Tia, or one of the teachers, what Raven did to you."

"No!"

"But it was wrong! We ought to report it."

"That will just make matters worse." Megan trembled. "I'm not like you, Carrie. Raven scares me. Please, don't tell. Please," she pleaded in a low voice.

Carrie bit her lip. She wasn't sure what to do. She hated to upset Megan anymore.

"Okay," she said at last, "but if Raven slaps you again, I'm dragging her to Mrs. Delgado myself!"

The girls joined Tia, Beth, and Jillian in the clearing. A bright, dancing fire had been built in one of the large fire pits. They were glad to sit in its warmth. It was nearly dark now, and the brisk, autumn air was chilly.

Raven avoided them. Carrie saw her talking briefly to the twins.

As soon as the program began, the microphone quit working. Mr. Lee and one of the other teachers got up and fiddled with it, but nothing did any good. Fortunately, Mrs. Delgado and most of the rest of the participants had strong voices. The staff sang loudly about protecting the environment. The girls from the Pheasant and Quail cabins presented a hastily-rehearsed skit. One of the high school students recited a poem describing the gruesome trials of the ill-fated Donner Party. Two other counselors gave a brief martial arts demonstration. Carrie relaxed. Even Megan seemed to forget her troubles and enjoy herself.

Sean volunteered Carrie to lead a camp song. She didn't mind. She loved to sing, so it was no hardship. She taught everyone a round that she had learned that summer at girls camp. When it was over, Derek dared her to sing a solo. She grinned back at him and sang one of her brother's favorite Scout songs, "The Flicker of the Campfire." She finished with "Sipping Cider." To her surprise, there was enthusiastic applause.

"Encore! Encore!" yelled Kevin and Evan.

Carrie held up both hands. "No, thanks," she said. "Let someone else have a turn." She slipped back into the crowd. She could tell the program was nearly over. Mrs. Delgado began to give the closing remarks.

Carrie decided to get the bugle. She wanted to allow enough time to polish it and practice a bit. She didn't have any trouble finding her way. The lodge was in plain sight and the moon was full, bright enough to cast shadows. All the same, she wished she'd thought to bring along her flashlight. The shadows reminded her of the spine-tingling story that Raven told at lunch.

She tiptoed into the darkened building. She didn't have any idea where the light switch was. How was she going to see the bugle? She ran her fingers over the wall without success. Finally she stumbled into a square table. On top of it was a small ceramic lamp. She turned it on. Its dim light didn't seem to stretch very far into the corners of the vast hall.

Carrie made her way to the fireplace. She climbed up on the big stone hearth. The horn hung by its strap from a nail. She had to stretch to reach it.

She had just started back across the room when she heard a noise coming from Mrs. Delgado's office.

It puzzled Carrie. She'd been certain that everyone else had remained at the campfire. Who could be in the lodge? She hesitated at the foot of the staircase. Finally, curiosity got the better of her. She slung the bugle over her shoulder and crept slowly upward.

The office door was shut. Only muffled sounds came through it. She couldn't tell if it was a man speaking, a student, or a woman with a deep voice. She couldn't even tell how many people were in the room. Maybe it was just one person, speaking into the telephone. Somehow Carrie was sure it wasn't anyone who was supposed to be there! She gripped the bannister tightly.

The voice came through louder now. She could pick up whole words and phrases: ". . . good crop this fall . . . kids interfere . . . risk losing harvest . . . arrange another accident . . . soon."

Carrie frowned in the darkness. There was something sinister about that one-sided conversation!

The unseen speaker apparently moved closer to the door, because now Carrie was able to hear more.

"I haven't seen the map, not since...." There was a short silence, then the voice continued. "No, I am not going back to hunt for it! What if I dropped it in the ruins? That place gives me the creeps! It's like a city of the dead. Every time I go there, I half expect to catch a ghost looking over my shoulder. Besides, we've memorized the map already. We don't need it anymore." Another, longer, pause followed.

Suddenly the door opened and light spilled down the stairwell. Carrie fled.

Chapter 16

CARRIE SPED DOWN THE STAIRS and out the door, her heart beating fast. A cloud covered the moon's face. She could barely see where she was going but, in her panic, she ran on anyway.

Two arms reached out of the darkness and grabbed her by the shoulders.

Carrie screamed.

The beam of a flashlight shone in her face and Mrs. Delgado's gentle voice said, "Carrie, where are you going? What's the matter?"

Carrie struggled to catch her breath. At last she managed to tell Mrs. Delgado that she had heard somebody in her office.

"I was afraid they'd see me," she said, "and know that I was…"

"Eavesdropping?" Mrs. Delgado finished for her.

Carrie's ears burned. She hadn't thought of it that way. "I guess so," she mumbled.

"You mustn't get so easily upset, Carrie. I'm certain it was just one of our staff members taking the opportunity to use the telephone. There's nothing unusual, or frightening, about that," Mrs. Delgado said patiently.

"But why were they talking about a harvest?"

"I imagine a number of our teachers have gardens. Mr. Lee even does a little farming during summer vacation. He specializes in agricultural research."

Carrie's face grew hotter. Why hadn't something like that occurred to her? After all, her own family ran a lawn care and landscaping business. She flexed her work-roughened hands. She had weeded a few gardens herself.

Mrs. Delgado lighted Carrie's way back to her cabin. "By the way," she said. "I enjoyed your singing during the campfire. Everyone did."

Carrie blushed again, but this time it wasn't from embarrassment. "Thank you," she said.

She slipped into her cabin. Tia and Beth were the only ones there. Carrie greeted them, and then rummaged through her cupboard. There were several things she needed to do within the next half hour.

She lay down on her bed with her journal. She wrote several labored sentences describing the day's activities. Afterward she drew a rough sketch of the ghost town. She paused for a moment, twirling the pencil between her fingers. She thought about the map that hung on the wall in Mrs. Delgado's office. Was that the other map that Sean wanted to investigate? She was almost positive it was a map of Haunted Ridge. Maybe Sean wanted to see if it showed any of the landmarks drawn on the map she had found.

Carrie shut her journal. She picked up her Book of Mormon and opened it to verse eight in the eighteenth chapter of Mosiah. Her mom had marked the place for her. Normally she listened to the scriptures on tape. However, since she couldn't bring her tape recorder to camp, her father had challenged her to practice reading them. He promised he'd do the same while she was gone. She rubbed the back of her neck. Her dad had dyslexia, too. This wasn't going to be any easier for him than it would be for her.

After asking the Lord to help her understand what she read, she put her bookmark under the first line. She slowly started deciphering the words. She had found in the past that it was better not to try to go too fast. Otherwise, the letters seemed to turn into black smudges that moved around on the page. To her relief, the phrases that she read were familiar. She was glad she had listened during family home evening.

"Carrie, you and Tia are reading the same book. How about that! I didn't know you two liked to read."

Carrie glanced upward. Beth leaned down from her top bunk. She looked with interest at the book in Carrie's hands.

"This is a great book," Carrie said. "I recommend it."

"What's it about?"

Tia answered readily. "It's a book of scripture, another testament of Jesus Christ. It tells about God's dealings with the ancient people who once lived on the American continent."

"Would you like to look at my copy, Beth?" offered Carrie. "I'm through reading for the night."

Beth stretched out her arm and Carrie placed the scriptures in her hand.

Megan had come in so quietly that Carrie didn't realize she was there until she spoke up. "My grandmother had a Book of Mormon. I can remember her reading it to me when I was a very little girl. I think my grandpa kept it after she died."

Tia's brown eyes sparkled. "I didn't know you were LDS, Megan."

"I guess I am," Megan replied. "Grandma had me get baptized when I was eight, but I don't recall much about it." She went over to examine the bugle that hung from the bedpost. "Are you going to play that tonight, Carrie? It's sort of dirty."

Carrie giggled. "That's tarnish, not dirt. I'll give the horn a good polish before I play it. All it takes is a soft cloth and a little elbow grease." She lifted the bugle down and pulled a baggy, blue T-shirt out of her storage cabinet. "Thank goodness my mom had me take this old shirt. Hopefully she won't mind if I use it. There's a hole in it anyway."

Carrie rubbed the instrument until it gleamed. She licked her lips and took a deep breath. She blew into the mouthpiece. High, clear notes filled the tiny cabin. Carrie closed her eyes and let her emotions soar with the music.

When she finished, Tia cleared her throat. "That sounded wonderful, Carrie, but it's a little loud for this small room. "Why don't you go out to the clearing?"

"Good idea. Is it ten o'clock yet?"

"Just about."

Carrie slung the bugle over her shoulder. This time she grabbed her flashlight before she left. The staff hadn't put out the fire yet. It still smoldered in the fire pit, its ashes glowing against the dark earth. Carrie stood close to its warmth and played two more tunes before she closed with "Taps." She heard the dogs howling again, as if in mournful echo of the music. The sound made her think of Sean. She knew he still missed Toby.

She returned to the cabin afterward. For a while she talked to the other girls. She asked them if they knew what kind of crops grew around Haunted Ridge.

"I'm not thinking of the Christmas tree farm," she said. "It has to be something that's harvested in the early fall, when the camp's still in use."

All the blood drained out of Megan's face.

Carrie had never in her life seen anybody turn so pale. "Megan!" she cried. "Are you all right?"

Megan just stared at Carrie, her eyes huge and frightened.

Beth looked up from her reading. "What's wrong?" she asked.

"N-n-nothing," Megan stuttered.

"Are you sure? You don't look like you feel very well," Tia said in concern.

Jillian ignored Megan's obvious distress. "I heard there's an apple orchard not far from here," she said. "Apples are harvested in the fall."

Carrie remembered Miss Higginbotham's gnarled old trees. How could they have anything to do with the camp's problems? They were ancient, and the trouble on Haunted Ridge had started just a few years ago. She rubbed her thumbnail against her lower lip. On the other hand, maybe there was something buried on the old woman's property. Carrie thought for a moment, then shook her head. Surely it had to be something more sinister than that to upset Megan so badly. What could it be?

She started to ask Megan about it, but the other girl burrowed deep under her blankets and pretended not to hear.

Raven had so little to say that Carrie wondered uneasily what she was plotting. Fortunately, Raven's bedding had dried in the sun. It still smelled faintly of Jillian's perfume, though. Raven made Jillian trade her pillows.

Before long, Carrie's eyelids grew heavy. She waited until the room was quiet, then she and Tia knelt together on the plank floor. After they said their prayers, Carrie jumped back into her warm sleeping bag. That night she dreamed of the broken chimneys and crumbling buildings in the abandoned town.

When morning dawned, Carrie's hand automatically reached out to shut off her alarm. It took her a moment to realize she wasn't at home in her own bed. The alarm hadn't woken her. The insistent noise she heard was a woodpecker. He was busy pounding holes in the trunk of a pine tree behind the cabin.

Tia was already up and dressed. She roused everyone else.

Jillian moaned, groaned, and whined, until Raven yelled, "Shut up!" and Tia threatened to give her extra kitchen duty.

The air was bone-chilling, shivering cold. Carrie dressed quickly. She zipped up her sweatshirt, then put her jacket on over it. Megan helped her wrestle with the left sleeve.

"It's a g-g-good thing this c-c-coat's about two sizes too big," Carrie said, her teeth chattering. "Otherwise I'd never g-g-get it on over my c-c-cast." She stamped her feet to warm them.

Jillian sprinkled jasmine-scented perfume all over herself. Within moments, the whole cabin smelled like a field of flowers.

Raven scowled and held her nose. She tried on first one shirt, then another, before deciding on a black sweater. She slid a glittering, deep-red bracelet onto her arm. The unusual bangle glistened like blood on her wrist.

Raven hogged the tiny mirror for so long that Carrie gave up waiting for it. She pulled a comb through her dark brown curls without looking at her reflection.

Tia straightened her braids, then offered to fix Megan's hair. She picked up a brush and set to work, coaxing the tangles out. She brushed Megan's hair until it shone like pale gold. Carrie was amazed at the results. Now it framed Megan's fine features, instead of hiding them.

"I don't know why you bother," grumbled Raven. "I can't see much improvement."

"Well, I like it!" Beth exclaimed. "Tia, you're an artist!" She ran the fingers of both hands through her own heavy waves of hair. "How about doing mine this afternoon?"

Tia laughed. "I don't recall hearing that hair-styling was part of a counselor's duties," she said, "but I'll see what I can do after lunch."

The girls stopped to wash up before heading to the kitchen.

Raven leaned close to Carrie as she dried her hands. "A lot of people in camp think you're the one who wrecked our cabin yesterday," she whispered.

"So I've been told." Carrie stared straight in front of her. She felt uncomfortable even talking to Raven.

"I think I can prove to them that it was someone else."

Carrie spun around to face Raven. "Really?" She gaped at the other girl in astonishment. "Why would you want to do that?" she asked. She'd thought Raven was the one spreading the rumors.

"I'm sorry about what happened down at the creek," Raven replied. "I'd like to make up for it."

Carrie felt almost giddy with relief. She'd expected trouble from Raven. An apology was a welcome surprise.

"There's just one little, tiny thing I'd like you to do for me in return," Raven said in a soft, silky voice.

"What did you have in mind?" Carrie asked warily.

Chapter 17

"ASK DEREK GRAHAM TO MEET YOU in front of the lodge at midnight," Raven pleaded, "then let me go in your stead."

Carrie blinked in surprise. "Why?"

"I just want to talk to him. Please, Carrie, help me out. I'd like to be his friend," said Raven. "He hasn't exactly seen me at my best." She twisted her bracelet around and around her wrist.

"Why do you have to wait until the middle of the night to make your peace with Derek? Do it during breakfast."

Raven rolled her eyes. "I can't do that right out in front of everybody," she said impatiently.

Carrie hesitated.

"What's the matter? Don't you think that Derek can take care of himself?"

"Yes, but..."

"Please," Raven begged again.

"Honestly, my influence over Derek isn't nearly as strong as you think it is," Carrie said.

"You could talk him into it if you tried. I know you could," Raven insisted. "Do this for me, and I'll make sure that the rumors stop. We could be friends." She cocked her head to one side. "I found out who was really responsible for ruining my things. Don't you want to see them punished?"

Carrie gnawed on her lower lip. It sounded so easy, a simple way to solve her problems. She was tempted to do as Raven asked. For a moment she wavered.

"After all, what harm could it do?" Raven coaxed in a sly voice.

Carrie thought of her desire to make new friends. The cost of this friendship was too high, she decided. Reluctantly she shook her head.

"You know the counselors aren't supposed to be meeting students after lights-out. Even if he'd agree to it, I can't ask Derek to break the rules. It's not fair to risk getting him in trouble just to bail myself out." Carrie dug her nails into the palms of her hands. "If you want to talk to Derek, do it on your own time!"

Raven's face set into hard, ugly lines. "You'll be sorry," she said fiercely. "I'll make you wish you'd stayed home!" She shoved Carrie against the sink, then stalked out of the washroom.

Carrie walked slowly to the kitchen. The other girls were already there, along with the boys from the Gray Foxes cabin. The chief cook, Mr. McHugh, was a tall, portly man with a white chef's hat atop his head. He helped Carrie remove her coat, then handed her an apron and hair net. She awkwardly tucked her unruly curls up under the net. After Megan tied the apron for her, Carrie started greasing the griddles Mr. McHugh had given her. She worked in silence. Her thoughts were still in a turmoil. Did Raven really know who had vandalized their cabin? Who could it be? Was it someone she knew?

Megan stood at the cutting board, scooping out cantaloupes. Raven and Beth carried trays to the tables outside. Tia stacked fresh blueberry muffins onto a platter.

Carrie scraped the leftover rinds and seeds into a garbage pail for Megan. Jillian came up and spoke quietly in her ear.

"What'd you do to Raven last night? I've never seen her so angry."

Carrie quietly told her about yesterday's incident at the creek.

Jillian gasped. "Raven's never going to forgive you for embarrassing her in front of Derek!" she exclaimed.

"I didn't embarrass her," Carrie answered indignantly. "She did that all by herself! Besides, what was I supposed to do? Let her push me in the brook?" She went over to the walk-in refrigerator and brought out several dozen eggs.

"Most of us have learned to either stay on Raven's good side, or stay away from her," Jillian commented. She flicked a melon seed off her pink-flowered shirt.

Carrie began cracking the eggs one-handed into a huge mixing bowl. Jillian hovered at her side.

"Listen, Carrie," she said, "Raven can be a lot of fun. You just have to do whatever she wants."

"Sometimes what she wants isn't right!" Carrie retorted.

Jillian shrugged. "Do it anyway. Otherwise, she'll make your life real miserable."

Carrie continued cracking eggs. "Is that what she does to you?" she asked. She studied the other girl while she worked.

Jillian fidgeted under Carrie's gaze.

Carrie's eyes narrowed. "Raven asked you to talk to me, didn't she? She told you what to say."

Jillian stepped backward. "How did you..."

"Just a lucky guess. Relax, Jillian, it's not your fault Raven thinks she has to control everyone. You can make your own choices." Carrie swept the egg shells into the trash. When she looked up, Jillian was gone. Sean stood in her place.

His eyes twinkled. "Bet you didn't know I'd been promoted to Mr. McHugh's second assistant." He smiled at Carrie and Megan. "Where's the bugle?" he asked.

Carrie grinned back at him. "It's hanging on my bedpost. Somehow the kitchen didn't seem the place to play it."

"Could you get it now? Mrs. Delgado needs you to let everyone know it's time to rise and shine. Megan and I can cook the pancakes."

"Why?"

Sean's expression grew serious. "The school bell's gone," he said. "Someone stole it during the night."

"You're kidding!" Carrie shook her hair free of the net. She tore off her apron and dashed out of the kitchen. Sure enough, she could see that the bell no longer hung from the fir tree. The branch was bare.

Carrie's heart started thumping. That tree was only a few yards from her cabin! It scared her to think of someone sneaking through the camp at night. She crossed the clearing in a daze. She had all but forgotten Raven's threats until she drew near a small group of students. They stopped talking and stared at her as she passed by.

Carrie tensed. She had the awful feeling that their conversation had been about her. "I didn't do it!" she wanted to scream at them. Instead she lifted her chin and pretended not to notice. She walked off with her head in the air.

Mrs. Delgado met her at the cabin door. "I see Sean already spoke to you," she said, forcing a smile. There were new lines of worry around her eyes. She thanked Carrie, then headed off in the other direction, muttering to herself as she went.

Carrie wondered uneasily what else had gone wrong that morning. If Mrs. Delgado hadn't been in such a hurry, she would have asked the camp director.

Carrie slung the horn over her shoulder and marched to the middle of the clearing to play "Reveille." Afterwards she went back to the kitchen to help dish out breakfast.

When she finally had a chance to sit down to eat, she noticed some of the staff members whispering among themselves. What were they talking about? Derek watched them with an alert expression on his face. Carrie remembered the suspicions he had voiced the night before. She drummed the fingers of her right hand on her knee. They certainly didn't suffer from a scarcity of suspects! There had to be some way to narrow the field.

Carrie decided to try talking to Megan again. She was convinced that somehow the other girl held the key to unlocking the mystery.

She nudged Beth. "Where's Megan?" she asked.

Beth shook her head, her mouth full of pancakes and bacon.

"I don't know," Tia answered for her. "At mealtimes Megan barely swallows enough food to hold body and soul together. She disappears before the rest of us have taken more than a bite or two." Tia twirled one of her long braids. "I'm worried about Megan," she said. "Something's bothering her."

Beth choked down her last bite. "I saw her walking toward the lodge," she managed to say.

"Thanks. I'll see if I can catch up to her." Carrie wrapped some leftover blueberry muffins in a napkin and stuffed them in the pocket of her sweatshirt. After taking care of her jacket, she set out for the lodge at a brisk pace. She halted at the entrance, her hand on the door. Was Megan inside? Maybe she'd gone around to the back. Certainly their meeting place had seemed familiar to her last night, as if she had been there before.

Carrie ran around to the rear of the building.

Megan stood in the shade of a madrone tree, next to the fallen log. With her left hand she held up a large rectangle of crimson-colored silk. With her right she made a magical gesture. The scarf bobbed, wiggled, danced and squirmed, apparently of its own accord.

Carrie watched spellbound. The piece of silk seemed alive!

Megan knotted the scarf in the center. She grasped it by one corner. With another graceful gesture, she slowly raised the scarlet material. The scarf mysteriously untied itself before Carrie's astonished eyes.

"Wow!" Carrie exclaimed. "How did you do that?"

Chapter 18

"MAGICIANS SHOULDN'T TELL ALL THEIR SECRETS," Megan teased softly. "If we did that, it wouldn't seem like magic." Her thin face lit up. "That was a new trick I've been practicing for my grandpa. Did you like it?"

"Absolutely!" Carrie sat down on the log. "Do you know any others?" she asked in awe.

Megan reached into a paper bag for a deck of unusually decorated cards.

"I don't play poker," commented Carrie.

Megan giggled. "Neither do I." She held her right hand up in the air and released the cards one at a time, in rapid succession. They fell like a waterfall into her left palm. "These aren't playing cards," she explained. "They're exhibition cards. We sell them especially for fanning." She stretched her arm out with a flourish. This time the cards gradually made a fan, with no visible motion of her hand. She snapped her wrist. The fan closed in one crisp movement.

The fan slowly opened and then closed, over and over again. Each time it did, the design on the backs of the cards formed a new pattern. Carrie was amazed. She knew it must have taken a lot of practice to handle the cards with such apparent ease.

"Would you like to learn a little magic?" asked Megan. There was a confidence in her voice that Carrie had never heard before.

"You bet!"

Megan took out another pack of cards. She let Carrie select one before she shuffled them. She cut the deck into three different piles.

At Megan's direction, Carrie placed her card on the middle pile.

Megan touched the top card in each set, then gathered them all back up into a single stack. She tapped her forefinger against the side of the deck. The stack separated at the card Carrie had chosen. It was as if an unseen hand had cut the deck.

"You've GOT to show me how you did that!" Carrie exclaimed.

"Here's the secret." Megan showed Carrie a small packet.

"Salt?"

"That's right. I had some in my pocket. I let a little fall on the card you picked." Megan divided the cards back into three piles. "Here," she offered, "you try it."

Carrie touched the top of each pile. As she did so, she let a few grains of salt drop on the first card in the middle pile. She stacked the other cards on top of it. Just as Megan had done, she flicked her finger against the side of the deck. Sure enough, the deck broke at exactly the right spot.

"See," said Megan, "it's simple if you know how." She reshuffled the cards and placed them in her sack.

Carrie wrapped her arms around her knees. She'd had no idea the other girl possessed such extraordinary skills. Megan was certainly full of surprises! What else did she know? Carrie decided to try questioning her again. Maybe this time Megan wouldn't escape into silence.

"Why were you so upset last night when we started talking about farming?" she asked.

"Why do you ask so many questions?" Megan retorted.

One corner of Carrie's mouth lifted in a wry grin. "I can't help it. Sean says I was born with an extra-strong sense of curiosity."

Megan leaned against the boulder. "You never give up, do you?" she asked in a weary voice.

"No."

"I won't give you the answers you want," she said quietly, "so you can stop being so nice to me." Megan sighed. "I know you just feel sorry for me, anyway."

"What's that got to do with anything? I feel sorry for anybody who gets teased, even myself!"

"When was the last time anyone dared tease you, Carrie O'Brien?"

Carrie flushed, but she answered honestly. "On Thursday I wrote my name and most of my vocabulary words backwards. The boy sitting next to me noticed. He thought that was really hilarious, so he told my entire social studies class about it."

"You wrote your name backwards?" Megan repeated incredulously.

Carrie nodded. "I did," she admitted. "Mr. Duvall said he'd need a mirror to read my paper." She didn't know whether to laugh or cry. The memory was still too fresh in her mind. She scuffed the toe of her shoe in the dirt. "I'm sorry if I made you uncomfortable. If you don't feel like answering a bunch of dumb questions, that's okay. You've done plenty for me already."

"I have?"

Carrie looked down at her left arm. "You help me when my cast gets in the way," she replied. "You've stood up for me even though you were scared. Best of all, you taught me a magic trick that will entertain my little sister and might actually impress my older brother." Carrie smiled. "Now that's an accomplishment! Besides," she added cheerfully, "members of Christ's church ought to give each other a hand. Like it says in the Book of Mormon, we should be 'willing to bear one another's burdens.'"

Megan stared at Carrie. There was sadness in her wide, gray eyes. "What good would church be to someone like me? Why should God care what I do?"

Carrie was taken aback. At first she didn't know what to say. How could she answer that kind of despair? Silently she pleaded for the Lord's blessing. After a few moments she said, "Let me tell you three of the Young Women Values I learned at church. They help me whenever I feel discouraged or unsure of which way to go." She took a deep breath, then recited in a soft voice:

"I am a daughter of a Heavenly Father who loves me, and I will have faith in His eternal plan, which centers in Jesus Christ, my Savior.

"I have inherited divine qualities which I will strive to develop.

"I am of infinite worth with my own divine mission which I will strive to fulfill."

Carrie leaned over and touched Megan's hand. "You and I are each children of God," she said earnestly. "He knows us by name and

He loves us. He cares what we do because He wants us to live again with Him someday."

Megan's eyes sparkled with unshed tears.

Carrie felt a lump in her own throat. The Spirit bore witness to her that what she'd said was true.

After a short pause, she spoke again. "One time Sister Yoshito and I stopped by your house to invite you to come to church."

"That was you? Grandpa told me some Mormons wanted to see me."

"Why wouldn't you come out of your room to talk to us?"

"I was sure you wouldn't like me."

"Really? I thought it was because you'd already decided you didn't like us!" exclaimed Carrie. She grinned. "I guess we were both pretty silly."

Megan smiled shyly back at her. "I guess so," she agreed.

"Would you like to come to church with me next week? You don't live very far from our apartment. My folks will be glad to give you a ride."

Megan hesitated. "I guess so," she said at last. "Grandpa will let me do that. He didn't mind when Grandma went to her church meetings. He said she always came home happy."

Suddenly Carrie heard Tia shout her name. She looked up. Her counselor was calling to her from one of the lodge's upper windows.

"Mrs. Delgado's looking for you," Tia yelled. "She needs you to signal the start of the first class."

Carrie ran back to the clearing. She blew three loud blasts on the bugle. Afterwards, she followed Tia and Megan to the nurse's station. Mrs. Garnett gave a presentation on emergency first aid. Most of the information was familiar to Carrie. She'd heard it before at girls camp. She glanced at Megan. The other girl seemed deep in thought.

When that class ended, Carrie blew the bugle again. Tia led the students past the kitchen area to the east end of the camp property. Since Carrie had missed the last part of yesterday's hike, she'd never been to that part of the forest. She drew her breath in sharply. It was so beautiful!

The creek had changed direction. It flowed southward now, down a gentle slope. Broadleaf maple and California laurel shaded its banks. The leaves on some of the trees were already starting to turn the bright colors of autumn. Carrie listened. Above the sounds of the students, she could hear a robin's song mixed with the raucous chatter of a jay bird. In the distance she heard a dog's faint whine.

Mr. Lee waited for them in a cool spot, not far from the creek. He had set up his podium and folding chairs under the wide-spreading limbs of a ponderosa pine.

Carrie looked for Sean, but he was nowhere in sight.

"We will be discussing plant adaptation this morning," Mr. Lee announced. "Remember, I expect each one of you to take notes."

"Oh, no!" Carrie groaned. She'd forgotten to bring a pencil and paper to class. Now she couldn't even pretend to write down what Mr. Lee was saying. She hoped he wouldn't notice.

Mr. Lee held up a cinnamon-colored cone from a Douglas fir tree. He compared it to a pine cone and showed the students how they differed. He was in the middle of relating an old Indian legend when all at once he stopped. He looked straight at Carrie.

"Why aren't you writing?" he asked.

Raven's voice piped up from the back. "Haven't you heard? Carrie's illiterate. She can't even read a 'no trespassing' sign!"

Carrie gulped. "It's easier for me to remember what you say if I just listen," she tried to explain. Her face felt like it was on fire.

"That's not the way it works for most people," Mr. Lee said sternly. "Next time, I want to see your pencil moving. Understand?"

Carrie was too mortified to speak. She simply nodded.

Instead of dismissing them for free time after class ended, Tia called the girls in her group together. She marched them back to their cabin.

"We need to talk," she said after they'd all filed inside. "Raven says she has some disturbing news to report."

Chapter 19

"I *TOLD* YOU," growled Raven, "I want to talk to the camp director."

"Mrs. Delgado is busy," Tia replied. "Speak to me first. I'll decide if we need to bother her."

Raven scowled.

Tia put both hands on her hips. "We're waiting. You said it was important."

"It is!" Raven snapped. "Everyone else in camp knows what happened to our cabin yesterday. They all know Carrie was responsible. It's about time you did, too!"

"Don't make accusations without proof," Tia said firmly. "Do you have a witness?"

"I'm her witness," spoke up Megan. "I saw who d-d-did it."

Raven glowered at Megan. "You'd better be careful," she said in a dangerously soft voice.

Megan looked as if she was about to faint. She clutched the bedpost for support.

Carrie set the bugle aside. Her eyes darted from Megan to Raven and then back to Megan. She could think of only one way to explain their recent behavior. "It was both of you, wasn't it?" she asked. She crossed her arms and leaned back against the wall.

Megan nodded miserably.

The others stared in amazement.

Tia threw her hands up in the air. "Now I'm really confused!" she exclaimed. "Will somebody please tell me what is going on here?"

"Raven slipped out of class early yesterday and returned to the cabin," Megan whispered. They all had to strain to hear her. "So did I," she continued. "I waited behind a tree until Raven came back out. When I went inside to check on my magic supplies, I discovered the mess she'd made."

Raven started angrily toward Megan, but Tia blocked her way.

Megan took a deep, shuddering breath. "I emptied Raven's cupboard, then poured perfume and hair spray over her bedding. After that, I started cleaning up the rest of the stuff. Carrie's things were all I had time to take care of before the lunch bell rang. I was afraid to stay longer." She wrung her hands together. "I'm so sorry, Carrie!" she blurted out. "I didn't realize that would cast suspicion on you. I tried to apologize later to Raven, but she…she…"

"Shut up!" yelled Raven. "Shut up, or I'll tell them all about that great family of yours. You wouldn't like that, would you?"

Jillian giggled.

"I d-d-don't c-c-care," Megan stuttered. "I'm not going to let you bully me into blaming C-C-Carrie." She lifted her eyes to meet Tia's steady gaze. "I should have told you what happened right away, before we ate lunch." She swallowed hard. "I'm awfully sorry for what I did."

"Who's going to believe that pretty little confession?" Raven asked scornfully. She turned to the others. "We all know Megan's a loser. Her own father didn't even want her! He dumped her on her grandparents' doorstep and then disappeared. She hasn't seen him since."

"And Megan's mother is in jail," Jillian added smugly. She looked to Raven for approval.

Beth's mouth dropped open in shock.

Megan closed her eyes as if she couldn't bear to see the other girls' reactions.

Carrie felt like all the air had just been knocked out of her lungs. She didn't know what to say, or how to erase the shame and despair etched on Megan's thin face.

"Oh, Megan!" Tia said, her voice warm with compassion. "How difficult it must be for you to deal with a situation like that!" She slowly shook her head. "Obviously your father and mother made some bad decisions. They're paying a heavy price for that. However," she added, glaring at Raven and Jillian, "nobody with even half an ounce of Christian charity would think it was your fault!"

Megan's eyes flew open. She seemed surprised at Tia's sympathy.

"Tia's right," chimed in Carrie. "You're not responsible for your parents' mistakes."

Beth solemnly agreed.

"That's all very touching," Raven snarled. "It doesn't change anything, though. Jillian will vouch for me. She'll say I didn't leave class early. I sat next to her the whole time. She poked Jillian. "Tell them you saw me," she ordered.

Jillian hesitated. "I guess I did," she said. She rubbed her silver locket nervously between her fingers.

"Say it!" Raven commanded. "Say you saw me there the entire period."

"Stop hounding her, Raven," Carrie said in disgust. "Don't ask her to lie for you."

Raven dug her elbow viciously into Jillian's side.

Jillian winced. "It doesn't matter whether or not I saw Raven," she said. "I know Megan made up that crazy story."

"Why?" asked Beth. "Megan had nothing to gain from it." Her glasses slid down her nose. She peered over them at Jillian.

"She's trying to punish Raven, that's why! Megan has good reason to want to get even. I can prove it," Jillian said eagerly. She didn't notice the black fury rising in Raven's face. "Carrie knows what I'm talking about," she continued, the words spilling out of her mouth. "She and her friend, Derek, saw Raven hit Megan."

"Is this true, Raven?" Tia asked in an indignant voice. Carrie had never seen their counselor look so disturbed. "I think you'll be talking to Mrs. Delgado, after all. She takes a dim view of physical abuse. I'll wager she doesn't think much of lying, or blackmail, either!"

"You idiot!" Raven screamed at Jillian. "You've ruined everything!" She stormed out of the cabin in a rage. Jillian followed her, bleating apologies as she went.

Tia left to find the camp director.

Beth heaved a sigh. "I'm glad that's over," she said. She scooped up an armload of books. "I'm going to go get something else to read. Do either of you want to come with me?"

Megan sank down on the edge of her bed, as if her legs would no longer support the weight of her body.

"No, thanks," said Carrie. Megan didn't respond, so Beth headed for the lodge alone.

Megan looked up at Carrie. "I guess I'm in big trouble," she said quietly.

Carrie sat down beside her. "Well, you'll have to tell Mrs. Delgado what you did. She won't be very happy about it. I'm sure, however, she'll have a whole lot more to say to Raven." Carrie drummed the fingers of one hand against her knee. "That solves one small piece of the campground's puzzle," she said, "but it leaves a bunch of other things unexplained. We still have a mystery. We still have too many suspects. What should..." She stopped in mid-sentence. "Do you hear anything?" she asked.

"I think someone's crying."

"Let's investigate!" Carrie hopped off the bed and dashed out the door. She ran toward a narrow ravine about twenty-five yards south of their cabin.

Megan followed.

They discovered Jillian crawling around on her hands and knees at the bottom of the gully. She sobbed noisily.

Megan put her hand on Carrie's arm. "What's wrong with her?" she asked.

"I don't think she's hurt. She seems to be looking for something. I guess we'd better see what's wrong." Carrie slid down the embankment. "Watch out for poison oak," she called.

"What happened?" she asked when they reached Jillian.

Wisps of frizzy blonde hair clung to Jillian's tear-streaked face. She brushed them away with sweaty fingers.

"My locket is missing," she said, sniffling as she spoke. "It was a gift. I HAVE to find it!"

Carrie squatted down and examined the ground around her feet. "It's not going to be easy," she said. "This place is covered with plants. How in the world did your locket end up here?"

"Raven yanked it right off the chain, then threw it as far as she could," Jillian explained. She rubbed a raw, red mark at the back of her neck.

"I could help you hunt for it," Carrie suggested. "Maybe Megan will, too."

Megan hesitated. She glanced uncertainly at Jillian.

"Please," Jillian begged. "I swear I'll never say another word to anyone about your mother ever again," she added hopefully.

Megan's chin lifted. "You'd better not say anything to anyone anyway!" she burst out. "My parents' problems aren't your business, so you can just keep quiet about them!"

Carrie covered her mouth to hide a smile. Maybe Megan was finally learning to stand up for herself after all.

"Okay, okay." Jillian hastened to change tactics. "I'll tell you what. If you find my locket for me, I promise I'll tell Mrs. Delgado so much about Raven Blake that she'll get sent home before dark. How does that sound?"

"It sounds dumb!" Carrie said bluntly. She rocked back on her heels. "Just tell Mrs. Delgado the truth. Don't use your imagination, or you'll get us all into trouble."

Jillian hung her head. "Okay," she repeated meekly. She and Megan started looking beside the small stream of water that flowed toward the creek. The two of them climbed over moss-covered rocks and pawed through the gravel at the water's edge.

Carrie hunted among the cattails and purple thistle. She couldn't resist taking a moment to rub the cattail's brown, fuzzy spikes. They felt soft as velvet. After a while, she decided to concentrate on a patch of wild blackberries. It'd be just like Raven to throw the locket in the brambles! Carrie gingerly poked her hand through the thorny plants, hoping to catch the gleam of silver. As she searched, she thought about the snatches of conversation she'd overheard last night in the lodge. What did it mean? She wished she knew. Maybe if she could figure that out, she'd have the solution to the campground's mystery.

There was a rustle in the bushes not far from her. Carrie stopped to listen. Was that an animal nearby, or had somebody else come to help them?

Suddenly she heard a loud, crackling noise, like the sound of a stick striking wood. She jumped to her feet. What was going on?

Chapter 20

CARRIE SOON FOUND OUT. Dozens of small yellow- and black-striped bodies swarmed through the air.

"Wasps!" Jillian screamed in terror.

Carrie leaped forward. "We've got to get out of here!" she shouted to Megan.

Carrie and Megan pushed and tugged Jillian up the bank, then swatted frantically at the wasps who were attracted to her heavy perfume and bright, flowered T-shirt. Jillian didn't help them much. All she did was wail. Her panic-stricken shrieks rang in Carrie's ears.

Tia and Beth met them at the top.

"Go get the nurse," Tia ordered Beth.

"Hurry!" urged Carrie as Beth dropped her books and sped away.

The girls carried Jillian to safety. Tia had her lie down as soon as they reached their cabin. Even though she had been stung only a few times, she seemed to be having difficulty breathing.

Carrie noticed that Jillian's right arm was already red and swollen. With Megan's help, she tied her handkerchief into a constricting band above the wasp sting.

Tia checked to make sure the band wasn't too tight. She slipped a pillow under Jillian's head and laid a light blanket on top of her.

Megan crouched down next to the bed. She stretched out her hand. In her palm was the silver locket.

"I found this under a fern," she said softly. "There wasn't time to tell you before we had to run from the wasps. I hope it makes you feel better."

Jillian gave her a weak smile. "Thank you," she said, her voice barely above a whisper. "I meant what I said earlier. I won't be telling any more of your family secrets. I promise."

Beth soon returned with Mrs. Garnett. The nurse put ice packs on Jillian's arm and gave her a strong dose of antihistamine. She complimented the girls on their quick response to a serious situation.

"Thanks to you," she said, "I think your friend will be all right. We'll take her to the hospital, shortly, just to make sure. Mrs. Delgado has gone to the lodge to phone her parents." Mrs. Garnett shooed them all outside so Jillian could rest.

Carrie grabbed the bugle on her way to the door. She hoped she would get a chance to play it again.

Once outside, Carrie paced back and forth. A crowd had gathered, drawn by all the noise. She spotted Raven and was careful to avoid her.

The back of Carrie's hand felt puffy and sore. Unconsciously she rubbed it.

"Did you get stung, too?" Megan asked. She held up her own hands. Two fingers were swollen to nearly twice their normal size.

Carrie winced. "Ouch," she said.

"Ouch," agreed Megan with a lop-sided grin.

Mr. McHugh came bustling up, his apron flapping. "Try this," he said. He gave each of them a saucer filled with a thick, white paste. "I mixed some baking soda with a little water. It'll draw out some of the pain."

The girls thanked him as they smeared the concoction on the places where they had been stung. It soothed them almost immediately.

Kevin and Evan watched. Their faces and hands were stained with juice.

"I see you found some ripe blackberries," observed Carrie.

Evan nodded happily.

Kevin peered curiously at Carrie. "How'd you stir up all those wasps?" he asked.

"I don't know," Carrie answered. She frowned. "It seemed like they just fell out of the sky."

"Not quite," Tia said in a grim voice. "There was a wasp's nest in one of the trees that hung over the ravine. Beth and I both saw someone hit it with a stick."

Carrie was horrified. "Who would do such an awful thing?" she asked.

"All I could see was the stick," Tia replied.

"I saw more than that," said Beth. "There was an arm at the end of that stick—an arm with a bright, red bracelet!" She pointed towards Raven.

Raven's eyes narrowed. "I'm not the only one in camp who wears jewelry," she said, "so don't look at me!" Her outward calm couldn't quite mask the fear on her sharp-featured face. "Beth's mistaken."

"I doubt it," responded Beth. "That bracelet is one-of-a-kind."

"You're just covering up for Carrie. She's responsible!" Raven claimed, her voice rising in anger. "You've got to tell everyone it's her fault!"

Carrie struggled to stay calm. Nothing could be gained by throwing a tantrum. Raven's accusations scared her, though. What if people believed them? The very thought made her furious.

Beth said, "Yesterday Tia told us that this kind of behavior wasn't Carrie's style. She was right. However, it is EXACTLY the mean sort of thing YOU would do, Raven. You knew Jillian was allergic to insect stings."

"No!" Raven yelled. "You heard me! Tell them Carrie did it. If you don't, I'll..."

"You'll do what?" interrupted Beth. "Blackmail me?" She pushed her glasses back up to the bridge of her nose. "Even if you did, I wouldn't lie for you. Carrie's my friend."

With a sense of shock, Carrie realized it was true. She HAD made friends here at camp. Beth, Megan, Tia, Jillian, Evan, and Kevin had all become her friends. It didn't matter to them whether or not she solved the campground's mystery. They were her friends because she treated them the way she wanted to be treated. Maybe that was Heather's secret.

Raven sputtered in rage. Her face turned an ugly shade of purple. The crowd of students drew back from her as if her fearful anger was a contagious disease. Everyone stared, but no one looked her in the eye.

Mrs. Delgado walked briskly over to Raven. "Collect your

things," she said. "You're leaving camp. I'll be contacting both your parents and the principal of San Angelo Junior High. I will expect Mr. Price to take disciplinary action."

"You can't do that!" Raven shrieked. She spun around and darted away into the forest.

Mrs. Delgado sent Mr. Lee and several other teachers after her. Tia followed them.

Beth announced she was going back to the ravine to get the books she had dropped. Megan offered to help.

The camp director sighed. "What a difficult day this has been," she told a remaining member of the staff. "I couldn't reach Jillian's parents. Our telephone's out of order."

Carrie overheard. "Do you mean that someone cut the lines?" she asked.

Mrs. Delgado gave her an odd look. "Your imagination is working overtime," she said. "Squirrels chewed through the wires. I understand that happens occasionally."

Carrie was skeptical. After all the trouble they had experienced, she thought it was much more likely that human hands were responsible!

Mrs. Delgado turned to leave. "I'm going to Miss Higginbotham's house," she said. "I'll ask to use her phone."
"Do you think she'll let you?" questioned Carrie.

Evan snorted. "That witch?" exclaimed Kevin. "Not likely!"

"Of course she will," Mrs. Delgado replied in a firm voice. "It's an emergency." She set off across the clearing.

Derek came up behind Carrie and spoke in her ear. "Have you seen Sean? He was supposed to meet me after the second class, but he never showed up."

"No. Maybe he's running an errand for Mrs. Delgado."

"He's not. I checked."

"Where could he have gone?" Carrie mused aloud.

"We know, we know," Kevin and Evan chanted in unison.

"You do? Derek asked in surprise.

Evan held his hand out.

"What will you give us?" his brother asked.

Derek's face darkened.

Carrie quickly stepped in front of the twins. "Look," she said, "a lot of spooky things have been going on around here. I'm worried. What if something's happened to my brother?"

"Oh, all right," Kevin said. "Sean took us on a hike. He thought you needed a break, Derek. Didn't he tell you?"

"Sure, he told me, but you two came back from the hike. He didn't." Derek's blue eyes darkened with worry. "What happened?"

"Nothing much," Kevin insisted. "Sean looked at the map in the lodge, then we climbed the ridge trail."

"Yeah, he said there was something he wanted to see up there," added Evan. "We ate berries on the way."

"So, do you know where Sean is now?" asked Carrie.

Evan shook his head.

"Not exactly," answered Kevin.

The muscles in Derek's jaw tensed.

Carrie knew he felt just as impatient as she did. "Please, tell us what you did on the hike," she asked.

"Right now!" ordered Derek.

"Don't get so excited," Kevin responded in an injured tone.

Evan shuffled his feet. "Like Kevin said, nothing much happened. We hiked up to the top of the ridge. Sean took a look at those red strips of plastic that mark the camp boundary line. He told us they were in the wrong place. He wanted to talk to Mrs. Delgado about it."

Carrie knew there was more to the story. "Then what?" she asked.

"Then we heard a dog," said Kevin. "It was tied to a tree a little farther down the other side of the mountain."

Evan said, "Sean went to check on it. He thought it might be hungry or hurt. We hurried back to camp."

"Didn't he want you to wait for him?" Carrie inquired.

"I don't know," Kevin said. "We didn't stick around to see. We just ran."

"We don't LIKE dogs," Evan confided.

"How much time has passed since the two of you last saw Sean?" Derek asked in a sharp voice. He scowled at them.

Evan shrugged.

"We're not certain," replied Kevin. "Maybe twenty minutes at the most."

"Not long," agreed Evan, "not long at all."

Derek's face cleared. "I guess I shouldn't have gotten upset so fast," he said. "I was afraid Sean'd been gone all morning."

Evan shook his head.

"We left late," Kevin confessed. "Mr. McHugh caught us throwing melon balls at each other during breakfast. He made us scrub the washrooms before we could go hiking. Yuck!"

"Sean helped us," continued Evan, "but it was after ten o'clock before we started up the mountain."

Derek clapped his hand to his forehead. "So that's why you missed the first aid class! Why didn't you tell me?"

The twins exchanged mischievous glances.

"We didn't think you'd want to hear about it," Kevin confessed.

One corner of Derek's mouth lifted in a reluctant smile. "You may have been right, Kevin," he admitted.

Evan grinned back at him.

"Hey!" yelled Kevin. "You can tell us apart."

Carrie gnawed her lower lip. She still felt concerned about her brother. Even though Sean had only been gone a short time, she was troubled by his absence. It was out of character. Sometimes Sean was over-confident, but he wasn't reckless. He knew he shouldn't wander around the woods alone. What if he'd gotten hurt when he tried to check on the dog?

"I've got a bad feeling about this," she said anxiously. "It's not like Sean. He wouldn't worry us on purpose. He should have caught up with the twins and returned to camp by now. We ought to find out what happened to him."

Derek's expression grew serious again. "You're right," he said.

Evan looked expectantly at Carrie.

"We heard that Carrie likes a mystery," said Kevin. "Why doesn't she figure it out for herself?"

Carrie met Derek's challenging gaze. "Fine, I will! Do you want to come with me?"

"I sure do! Let me get permission first. We'll meet back at the lodge." Derek left to locate one of the teachers.

With the twins at her side, Carrie went over to talk to Megan.

Chapter 21

CARRIE PACED BACK AND FORTH in front of the lodge. As she did, she prayed for Sean's safety. A nagging sense of urgency tugged at her mind. She was eager to get started. Now she understood how worried the others had felt when she'd turned up missing.

At last Derek arrived. A pair of field glasses hung from a strap around his neck.

"I had a hard time tracking down a member of the staff," he told Carrie. "They all seem to be busy elsewhere. I finally found the cook. He was in the storeroom, opening cans of tomato juice, but he gave us permission to hunt for Sean." Derek glanced at the horn that Carrie had slung over her shoulder. "Mr. McHugh said to blow the bugle if we run into trouble."

"Good," she said, tapping her foot. "Let's go."

Kevin and Evan stopped pelting each other with pine cones. They followed Carrie and Derek down the road towards the creek.

A pungent odor hung in the air. Evan sniffed.

"Ugh! I smell a skunk," Kevin said. He hurried on ahead.

When they came to the bridge, they discovered an immense cedar tree lying across the road. It blocked the way out of the campground. Most of the teachers were there, working to move it aside.

Mr. Lee waved.

Carrie waved back. For a moment she considered inviting him to join them, then decided against it. After the scolding he had given her in class, she was embarrassed to ask him to help look for her brother. Mr. Lee had already searched for her the day before. He'd probably conclude that getting lost was an O'Brien family failing.

Derek strode along the brook's edge. He led the others to the pond.

Carrie noticed that someone, most likely J. R. Golbin, had erected a makeshift barrier across the path to the ghost town.

"Where's Megan?" Derek asked as they began hiking up the ridge trail. "She usually sticks pretty close to you."

"I talked to her just before we left," Carrie answered. "She was afraid to come with us. There's something about this place that scares her and I can't get her to tell me what it is."

Evan patted Carrie on the back.

"That's okay," Kevin consoled her. "You still have us."

"But only until we meet a dog," Derek retorted. He noticed the look of bewilderment on Carrie's face as she looked around. "We're going the opposite direction of the way we went yesterday," he explained, "so you're seeing things from a different angle."

"Oh."

When the trail turned southward, Evan gestured toward an overgrown path beyond the fluttering, scarlet boundary flags.

"Here's where we left Sean," Kevin announced. He and Evan seemed nervous.

Carrie knew it reminded them of the dog.

Derek nudged her. "They're right. Your brother went that way." He pointed out a small cluster of stones that formed the shape of an arrow. "We learned to leave signs like that at Scout Camp."

Carrie called Sean's name, but there was no answer. She brushed past the twins.

"Come on," she urged.

The four of them took the narrow, little-used path up the slope. They had to duck under pine limbs and push branches away from their faces. Soon they reached the top of the ridge. They peered down into the valley below.

To their right, Carrie glimpsed the apple orchard and Miss Higginbotham's cozy, yellow cottage. Beyond that lay the ruined city. Zeke and Harry's barn and run-down cabin were straight ahead, at the foot of the mountain. A tangle of tall trees and bushes almost obscured the buildings. Two scrawny German shepherds prowled restlessly behind a wire enclosure.

Carrie's brow furrowed in thought. Not once had she seen any fruit trees or gardens on the camp property. Behind her was nothing but natural forest growth. So why did someone fear the students would interfere with their harvest? Why was someone going to such extraordinary lengths to close the campground? Were they hiding something illegal?

The trail veered sharply to the left, around two trees that leaned together in a leafy embrace. The sight jogged Carrie's memory.

"Wait, Derek," she said. "Didn't that map I found have a drawing of two trees on it?"

"That's true. It did." Derek's brow furrowed. "Say, where is that map?"

"Sean has it," Carrie replied. "He thinks those X's mark places where gold is buried. I'm positive he's wrong."

Evan hopped up and down in excitement.

"Gold!" exclaimed Kevin.

"No," disagreed Carrie. "I'm afraid it's something much more dangerous."

Derek frowned at her. "Why? What else could the X's stand for?"

"I'm not sure," Carrie admitted. She felt frustrated. She was certain the solution to the mystery of Haunted Ridge lay within her grasp, if only she could fit the pieces of the puzzle together.

She and Derek walked over to investigate the trees. The twins hung back.

A rope dangled from an upper branch. The earth underneath it was scuffed by many footprints. There were signs of a struggle. Lying in the dirt was another piece of rope.

Carrie picked it up. A few dog hairs still clung to its frayed edge.

Derek lifted the binoculars to scan the area below them. Almost immediately, his body stiffened.

"What's the matter?" Carrie asked anxiously. "What do you see?"

Derek handed her the binoculars. "Look down there," he said, "at the old shack."

Carrie's hands were still a little sore. She held the field glasses awkwardly, but at last she saw what Derek meant. What had at first looked like a pile of clothes on the cabin's front porch, was topped by flame-red hair. It was Sean!

She thrust the binoculars back at Derek and raised the bugle to her lips.

Derek grasped her wrist. "Don't," he said. "Not yet. I don't like the look of this. We'd better find out what's going on before we make a lot of noise."

"But we need to get help," Carrie argued. She wished desperately now that she had asked Mr. Lee or one of the other adults to come with them.

"I agree." Derek jerked his thumb towards the twins. "Send them."

Carrie dashed back to Kevin and Evan. "I need you two to do something really important for me. Do you think you can?"

"Of course," said Kevin.

"Whatever you want," added Evan.

"Good. Go back to camp. Tell the teachers we located Sean. He's at Zeke and Harry's place." Carrie swallowed hard, past the lump in her throat. She took a deep breath. "He might be hurt," she continued. "Tell them to hurry over there right away!"

Evan saluted smartly.

"We're on our way," said Kevin.

Suddenly the dogs howled, a long, keening cry that totally unnerved the twins.

The two boys bolted. They crashed pell-mell through the forest undergrowth until they reached the ridge trail. They turned to the right and vanished from sight.

"Darn it!" Derek groaned. "They're taking the long way back. I wish I could send you!"

"Don't even try. I'm not leaving until I make sure Sean's all right," Carrie said stubbornly. She turned her back on Derek and continued on until she came to a big stump. She halted. This might be another one of the landmarks on the map.

Derek started forward, but she put her hand out, blocking his way. "Hold it," she said. She lifted a heavy stone and tossed it into the pile of leaves on the path next to the stump. The leaves disappeared in a cloud of dust, revealing a deep hole.

Derek gawked at the pit in horrified surprise.

"It's a trap," Carrie explained matter-of-factly. "Those X's marked hazards, not treasure." She stared straight ahead. There, twenty yards away, grew the reason for the problems they'd been having. "I know now who's responsible for all this trouble," she said. "It's somebody who wants to keep visitors off this side of the mountain. That's why they moved the boundary flags close to the top of the ridge—so that people would think the camp property ended there, and stay away."

As she finished speaking, Carrie felt a hand on her shoulder. She nearly jumped out of her skin in fright.

Megan stood beside her. Neither Carrie nor Derek had heard her approach.

Carrie heaved a sigh of relief. "You scared me half to death!" she exclaimed.

Megan struggled to get her breath. Evidently she had run to catch up with them.

"There's something you should know before you go any farther," she gasped.

"It's about Zeke and Harry, isn't it?" Carrie asked soberly. "They're growing marijuana by their house."

"What?" Derek's jaw dropped. He was obviously shocked.

"Look," said Carrie. "You can see it."

Distinctive, emerald-green plants peeked through the brush surrounding the cabin. Now that the students had drawn nearer, the bright-colored weeds were easy to spot.

"My m-m-mother knew Harry and Zeke," Megan said. She put her face in her hands. "She t-t-told me once where they lived, and what they were doing. She said Harry's dangerous!" Megan looked up. Her eyes pleaded for forgiveness. "It's hard for me to talk about my mother and the people who used to visit her. I finally realized that I had to warn you, though. Hiding the truth put you in danger."

Now Carrie understood the reason for Megan's fears and her reluctance to answer questions. She nodded sympathetically.

"It finally dawned on me that Harry had to be involved in the campground's problems," she said. "The trouble began after he moved here. I'm certain he caused Mr. Golbin's accident. He and his partner must have been frantic when they found out the camp was reopening this fall. They were afraid that someone would discover their illegal crop, or interfere with its harvest. The two of them kept offering their help so we wouldn't suspect them. Didn't you notice they were always on hand whenever anything went wrong?"

Derek's eyes glittered with wrath. He opened his mouth to speak, then closed it with a snap.

A door banged shut below them, followed by voices raised in anger. Zeke and Harry ran out of their house, slamming the door behind them. The sounds resonated in the thin mountain air.

Carrie desperately wanted to hear what the men were saying, so she moved closer and closer until she was crouched at the very edge of their property. "Lord, please protect my brother," she begged silently.

Derek joined her. "I sent Megan to Miss Higginbotham's house to call the sheriff," he whispered. "Help should be here soon. What should we do until then?"

Carrie raised her finger to her lips. "Listen," she whispered back.

"We have to get rid of that kid!" shouted Zeke. "We can bury him in the woods. He'll never be found."

"That won't work!" Harry roared back in scorn. "We'd have law officers and half a dozen search parties roaming all over our land."

"If we let him go, he'll tell." Zeke threw his hat on the ground. "Let's just get out of here. I never wanted to be part of this in the first place."

"Don't be a fool. You can't quit now! There's a way the kid won't talk and we won't get blamed."

"How's that?"

"We'll hold him face-down in the bath tub until he stops breathing. After that, we'll dump him in the pool behind the dam. Everyone will think he drowned there." Harry stroked his curly beard. He chuckled. "The parents will raise such a ruckus that the Golbins' campground will be shut down permanently. It's perfect!"

The contrast between Harry's jolly face and his callous words chilled Carrie. She shuddered.

"I don't like it," Zeke grumbled.

"You have no choice. Get the truck. I'll fill the tub." Harry stomped back inside.

Chapter 22

ZEKE HESITATED ON THE FRONT STEP. He couldn't seem to make up his mind whether or not to go along with Harry's plan.

Carrie started crawling forward.

Derek seized her ankle. "Stay here," he whispered. "I'll get Sean."

"No way!" Carrie protested in a low voice. "He's my brother! What makes you think I should sit and do nothing while you rescue him?"

"Do it for Sean's sake," Derek said softly. "One person can move faster and attract less attention than two. Besides, I don't even know if he's conscious. I might have to carry him. You couldn't help with that—not with a cast on one arm."

Carrie bit her lip. How could she bear to just watch? She knew Derek was right, however. He had a better chance alone. She vowed to see that both boys made it to safety.

"Okay," she said.

Zeke seemed to come to a decision, also. He walked toward a battered pickup truck.

Derek slipped quietly through the shrubbery.

On the front porch, Sean fought to sit up.

Derek crept to his side. Carrie could see him struggling grim-faced with the ropes that bound her brother.

The dogs sensed the presence of the newcomers and began to yelp. Zeke ignored the noise. He fumbled in his pockets for his keys.

At last Sean was free. He stood up and promptly toppled over. Derek picked him up with one swift movement, heaving Sean over his broad shoulders like a sack of potatoes.

The dogs' barking reached a frenzied crescendo.

Harry stuck his head out the window. "Shut those animals up!" he bellowed. "What's the matter with them?"

Zeke turned toward the cabin.

Carrie wanted desperately to flee. Instead she jumped to her feet and blew the bugle.

Harry cracked his head on the window frame.

"Get the gun!" Zeke cried.

"No!" Harry hollered, clutching his head. "Bullet wounds would be too hard to explain. Set the dogs on her!"

Carrie waited, her stomach churning with fear, until Sean and Derek had slipped out of sight. As soon as she was sure they had escaped, she ran for her life.

Zeke flung open the door to the pen. The dogs charged after Carrie.

A mind-numbing panic threatened to overwhelm her. She choked it down and prayed for guidance. She couldn't outrun Zeke and the dogs. She'd have to out-think them. Rather than trying to find her way back to the ridge trail, she sped northward along the base of the mountain, toward the ghost town. She could see it in the distance, its chimneys and ruined buildings rising out of the field.

The dogs snapped at her heels. She wrenched the leftover muffins out of her pocket and flung them over her shoulder. The half-starved beasts immediately forgot all about her as they fought over the scraps of food.

Carrie dropped down between two evergreen bushes and struggled to catch her breath. She hoped Zeke wouldn't figure out where she was now that the dogs were busy.

The man yelled and cursed, trying to force the dogs apart. One of the German shepherds turned on him. The animal snarled and showed its teeth. The fur along the back of its neck bristled as it advanced. Carrie saw the expression on Zeke's face change from anger to alarm. He galloped away with the dog in pursuit.

Carrie slithered out of her hiding place.

The remaining dog licked the last crumbs off the ground, then bounded after her.

Carrie gasped in terror. She turned and scrambled straight up the mountain. Her feet slipped on the thick carpet of pine needles. She started to slide. She grabbed a branch, but it snapped off in her hand and she fell.

A menacing growl rumbled in the German shepherd's throat. Carrie inched backward, her eyes on the dog. Her heart beat like it was going to thump right out of her chest.

Then the dog leaped.

Carrie blew the bugle again. She hit the highest, shrillest, most earsplitting note she could reach. The dog squealed and spun around in mid-air. It ran whimpering in the opposite direction.

Carrie put her head in her hands and almost sobbed in relief. After a moment she slid the rest of the way down. She realized she was near the grassy track that led to the pond. She sighed, wishing she knew whether she should go to the right or to the left in order to return to camp.

She decided to continue on to the abandoned city. From there she was certain she could find Miss Higginbotham's house. Surely Megan was there and had already phoned for help. Carrie quickened her steps.

Suddenly she heard the ominous roar of an engine. It was Harry, driving his pick-up truck straight at her!

Carrie raced for the ghost town. She knew Harry would have trouble steering his vehicle through the mounds of debris there. She made it to the ruins five scant seconds ahead of the truck. Once there, she dove behind a crumbling wall.

The pick-up rolled to a stop, and Harry shut off the motor. Carrie heard him slam the door as he got out.

She bent close to the earth and tiptoed from one tumbled-down building to the next. She crouched down low. Could Harry see her? She cautiously raised her head.

He stood a few yards away. Nothing but a pile of broken, decaying boards separated him from Carrie. His features twisted in a ghastly smirk as he clambered over the planks.

She held her breath.

All at once the rotting wood collapsed beneath him. Harry didn't even have time to cry out before he dropped out of sight. There was a loud crash, then silence.

Nearly a minute passed before Carrie dared walk over and peer into the gaping hole. The figure at the bottom moaned, but didn't move.

The sound of heavy footsteps echoed through the rubble.

Carrie looked up to see Miss Higginbotham. The old woman held a shotgun cradled in her arms.

"Well," she said in her deep voice, "I see you caught one. Where's his partner?"

"Last I saw, he was being chased by one of his own dogs," Carrie answered.

"Never mind. I telephoned Sheriff Hoskins. He's on his way with medics and a whole slew of lawmen. They'll soon round up that young fool."

"Did you know what Zeke and Harry were growing?"

Miss Higginbotham's lip quivered. She hung her head.

"I had a pretty fair idea," she confessed. "Didn't think it mattered much. Always believed in leaving folks alone, long as they didn't bother me."

"My mom says we can't ignore evil," Carrie said seriously. "If we do, it'll never go away."

Miss Higginbotham shuffled her feet. "Guess your mom's wiser than me."

"Is my friend Megan still at your house?"

"That skinny, blonde-headed girl? Sure enough. She came barging into my place. Insisted I call the sheriff. Said her friends were in danger. Looked so scared, I thought she was going to pass out! She quaked like a leaf in the wind, but she wouldn't leave me alone until I telephoned."

Carrie grinned. "Good for her!"

The woman gave a snort of laughter. "I'll watch Harry here," she said. "Doesn't look like he's going anywhere soon. He can't be moved until the ambulance comes anyway. You go get your friend."

There was something else that Carrie was still curious about. "Miss Higginbotham," she said, "may I ask you one more question?"

"Humph! You can ask. Don't guarantee I'll answer!"

"Who's buried in that grave by the black oak tree?"

"Jerry," was the old woman's gruff reply.

"Jerry? Jerry who?"

"Jerry, my mule, that's who!"

Carrie blinked. That wasn't at all what she'd expected!

Miss Higginbotham cleared her throat. "He was a GOOD mule," she said defensively.

"He must have been," Carrie agreed with a smile. She went to find Megan.

Beth greeted the two of them upon their return to camp. "Hi!" she called out. "Did you hear what happened to Raven?"

Carrie and Megan exchanged glances. So much had happened in the last hour that they'd all but forgotten their problems with Raven.

"No," said Carrie. "Tell us."

"She ran into a bunch of skunks. Mrs. Delgado made her take a bath in tomato juice before she left. And that's not all! She's going to have even worse miseries when she gets home. She was standing right in the middle of a patch of poison oak when she stirred up those wasps. In her hurry to get away, she tripped and fell face down in the stuff."

Carrie had had poison oak before. She remembered how horribly it itched. For a second she felt sorry for the other girl, then she was struck by another thought. What if the whispers and rumors continued?

"Raven will try to get even," she said, her brows drawing together. "She's not going to stop telling lies."

Beth took off her glasses and wiped them on her shirttail. "Don't worry," she said. "I think we've all had enough of Raven by now. It'll be an awfully long time before anybody believes anything she has to say." Beth rubbed the bridge of her nose. "It's been such a strange day," she said in wonder. "The Thornberg twins came tearing into camp a couple of minutes ago, yelling that they had to see Mrs. Delgado. Do you know what's going on?"

"We had some trouble at Zeke and Harry's place. I guess I ought to go talk to Mrs. Delgado, too." Carrie forced her exhausted legs to move in the direction of the lodge.

The next day, Carrie convinced Megan to put on a magic demonstration. Evan giggled with delight when Megan pulled an egg from his brother's ear.

Carrie, Beth, Tia, Bee, Chou, Derek, and Sean applauded. Megan beamed.

Sean nudged Carrie with his elbow. "Would you like some good news?" he asked. There was a big smile on his good-natured face. He seemed none the worse for his ordeal in the woods. All that showed of his encounter with Zeke and Harry was a few bruises and a rope burn on one wrist.

Carrie felt a fervent prayer of gratitude in her heart as she gazed at her brother. Things could have so easily turned out different. Certainly God had watched over them both!

Her own mouth curved upward. "Of course," she responded cheerfully.

"Look who's here," said Sean. He pointed across the clearing.

Amy Noring stood at the end of the dirt road, her arms loaded with luggage.

Carrie ran to meet her. "Oh, Amy!" she cried. "I'm so glad to see you! What happened to your spots?"

"They're gone. The doctor said it was just an allergy," Amy answered. "I'll never have to eat brussels sprouts again in my whole, entire life." She handed one of her cases to Carrie. "Have you had fun so far?" she asked.

Carrie felt a huge grin spreading over her face. "It was a little more exciting than I expected," she admitted, "but once I stopped feeling sorry for myself, I made some new friends. Want to meet them?"

"Sure, but first you'd better explain about those ugly elves you expected to see here."

"The goblins? As a matter of fact, I guess you could say I actually did see a couple of them. They were wicked, Amy—you wouldn't have liked them at all! Last I heard, one was in jail and the other was under guard at the hospital."

Amy raised her eyebrows until they nearly disappeared under her light brown bangs. "Wow! Tell me all about it," she said eagerly. She linked arms with Carrie as the two of them walked towards the small, happy group surrounding Megan.

About the Author

Janna Goodman is a busy mother of seven who enjoys spinning an exciting tale of mystery and intrigue.

Her goal is to provide quality reading for youth. "There is a growing need," she observes, "for wholesome, worthwhile books for young readers. Storytelling is a valuable tool for teaching gospel principles to our children. Since I love to tell stories, I hope to be able to make a contribution in this field of endeavor."

Janna and her husband, Glenn, live with their family in Yuba City, California, where they both serve as stake missionaries. Among her favorite pastimes are learning, writing, reading, needlework, and collecting old glassware and second-hand jewelry. Janna studied elementary and special education at Brigham Young University.